The battle

that was fought that night probably had no parallel in the history of the world.

The attacking fleet consisted of the *Segomay 8*—a thousand-foot-long sea-mining maintenance freighter from the twenty-ninth century—a fishing vessel from the forty-third century, a space research ship from about A.D. 10,000, a pleasure yacht from the Clen civilization of around A.D. 13,000, a small craft with one male from the two-hundredth century, AND a submarine—the U.S.S. *Sea Serpent* commanded by William Kenlon—from an early, primitive mechanical era.

The enemy was a *single* supership from a civilization that had its home planet in the Milky Way.

THE
WINGED
MAN

—◆—

by
A. E. VAN VOGT
and
E. MAYNE HULL

D A W   B O O K S ,   I N C .
Donald A. Wollheim, Publisher

1633 Broadway
New York, N.Y.   10019

Cover art by Douglas Beekman

First DAW printing, March 1980

1 2 3 4 5 6 7 8 9

Chapter 1

In the darkness, the bird swept the submarine from stem to stern, swooping along almost at deck level and about a dozen yards to port. It was an enormous shape; and Kenlon, who saw the movement of it against the clouded sky, turned and watched it swerve away and vanish, flying strongly, into the northwest.

Kenlon glanced questioningly at Quartermaster Reichert, who was busy with the electric steering gear. But the man seemed not to have noticed the strange bird's passage. Once again, Kenlon faced in the direction the bird had taken. He said under his breath:

"Wrong direction, birdie! If you want to stay alive, the route is not in the direction of Tokyo. In fact—"

He stopped, frowning. Funny, he thought, *funny!* He picked the phone out of its waterproof box.

"Tedders speaking," said the voice of Lieutenant Tedders.

"It's a game I'm playing," said Kenlon. "And I ran out of fingers to count. How far are we from the nearest land?"

"You awaken me, sir," said Tedders indignantly, "out of the soundest sleep I've had in weeks—"

Kenlon grinned. There was a standing lottery among the crew members, which would be won by the first man who, when sent to rouse Tedders for special duty, found him asleep. The *Sea Serpent's* third officer had the astonishing faculty of waking up a few seconds before he was called.

No one had ever seen him nodding when he was on duty. He was on duty now.

Tedders finished his plaint; then: "In response to your question, Mr. Kenlon, the Pacific is perhaps the largest body of ocean in this hemisphere, and the U.S.S. *Sea Serpent*, heading out from base on the longest trial run of its short career, is now some twelve hundred miles from the nearest known atoll. Maybe that's a little exaggerated."

"Dazzle me further," Kenlon coaxed, "with your knowledge. String me off quite casually the names of all the large birds you know of that can fly twenty-four hundred miles."

"We-e-l-ll, there's the albatross."

He paused, and Kenlon urged: "Yes, yes, go on."

"See here," Tedders said irritably, "I'll have you know that when the Korean War began, back there aways, I was just getting comfortably settled into a large chair with a cushion in the firm of Carruthers, Carruthers, Tait, and Carruthers, who are *not* ornithologists. No one will ever be able to give me a rational explanation of why, after the war was over, I decided to stay in the service and spend the rest of my life in a mechanical sewer pipe under the sea."

"Albatross," Kenlon mused aloud. "That's a chap with a twelve- to fourteen-foot wing spread?"

"That's right."

"With a long, strong bill, hooked at the end?"

"Huhuh!"

"Fourteen feathers in its rounded tail and very narrow wings?"

"You're getting awfully warm."

"You'll have to do better than that," Kenlon announced. "That isn't the one. The one I saw had an eighteen-foot wing spread, with rather wide wings—"

"Maybe it's the daddy of all albatrosses."

"—no bill, no tail feathers at all," Kenlon went on, "and a body that seemed awkwardly large even for that wing spread. Question: Do bats grow to the size of small airplanes?"

"Question," said Tedders. "Do first officers go batty after they've spent a certain amount of time each night above the hatch? Or is this a case of too much *down* the hatch from a secret supply of joy juice?"

Kenlon, who never drank, frowned. He had, he knew, no business being offended, since it was he who had started the little byplay. To be practically told, however, that he was mentally disembarked, was hard taking. He said curtly:

"I'll make further observations, Mr. Tedder, and this time I shall wear glasses."

He hung up, and stood there in the darkness, staring up into the night sky. The clouds had thickened where the bird had disappeared, but to the southwest, where the moon rode behind white cumulus, there were patches of blue sky, from which starlight flickered.

Up in those heights a wind must have been blowing. Because abruptly the moon swam into one of the dark-blue windows. Its light streamed from an opening that widened rapidly. Through the expanding channel, the white moon rays poured down over the submarine and fired the intensely black sea with a lane of light.

A shadow darkened the face of the moon. Kenlon, on the verge of turning away, glanced up again. Then he gasped. And caught at the railing with tense fingers.

Plainly silhouetted against the moon was the figure of a tall man with wings. The wings were only partly spread; and they were not moving. He seemed to be poised there like a creature out of a nightmare, black as only a shadowed outline can be. Intently he stared down toward Kenlon.

For a long instant, that was the picture, like a "still" taken at night. And then, the legs drew up, the body lost its manlike appearance.

A great bird swooped out of the path of the moon into the covering darkness.

The minutes trickled by. The long, gleaming supership rolled and hissed through the slow swell, a monster surging at speed through a dark sea.

The atomic-powered steam turbines maintained their strong forward drive. A head poked up through the hatch.

"May I come up, Mr. Kenlon?" said Tedders.

Kenlon nodded. "What is it?"

Tedders climbed up beside him. "I've been thinking," he said, "of birds with eighteen-foot wing spreads, of an officer named William Kenlon who is famed for his snap judgments as to distance, and whose estimates of the length of ships seen a mile or more away are final. And lastly I've been thinking very hard indeed of a certain guy named Tedders, who isn't bright enough to realize when a conversation is serious." He broke off. "You actually saw that bird?"

It was an apology. Which meant that Kenlon's final words on the phone had shown his pique.

Kenlon hesitated. He went over in his mind the words he would have to use to explain exactly what his last visualization had been. And shook his head ever so slightly.

"It was dark," he said, "and it was over there"—he pointed into the night—"and all I really got was an impression."

"Aeronautically speaking," said Tedders, "I'm only a lightweight. I almost joined the air force—almost meaning that they turned me down flat. But could it possibly have been a very slow, small plane? Some kind of an observational plane? After all, a lot of people would like to know just what we've got here."

Kenlon did not reply immediately. And it wasn't that he considered the other's argument worth thinking about. It was Tedders' assumption that he had been deadly serious on the phone that brought the startled realization—that he had been.

He thought intensely: What did I see? A manlike bird with a wing spread of eighteen feet!

He found himself, uncertainly, wondering if some country had succeeded in inventing wing attachments for human beings.

It was a new idea completely; and it took a minute to fix the mechanical problems of such an invention in his mind.

He came out of the brief reverie with the conviction

that he had better say as little as possible. He mustered a grin, and stared down at the dapper Tedders.

"A plane of that kind away out here?" he said incredulously. "Besides, a plane would have registered on our instruments; but there have been no reports. Apparently, I was the only one who saw it, and even I'm not sure—"

"Mr. Kenlon."

It was Quartermaster Reichert. Kenlon half-turned, startled by the interruption.

"Yes?" he said.

"Did you send somebody down to the end of the for'ard deck, sir?"

"Did I what?" Kenlon asked.

He twisted. Then he was down on the deck, racing along toward the shape that was clinging to the prow. He could hear Reichert's heavy footsteps close behind him; and, somewhere in the rear, Tedders was shouting muffled commands down the hatch.

As Kenlon approached, the winged man looked up. In the darkness, his great eyes shone like dull jewels. It was too dark to make out the features of his face, or even the contours of his body.

All that mattered, all that Kenlon concentrated on after one flashing look, was that the birdman was in some way fastening what looked like a brassy pie tin to the outjutting edge of the prow of the *Sea Serpent*.

The metal thing shone and danced with streaking flashes of dimly reflecting light from a now partially hidden moon. Above it towered the crouching man, his monstrous wings flapping from well down behind his shoulder blades.

And he didn't move. He clung there, with a curious desperation, and pressed his metal pan against the metal of the submarine—as Kenlon vaulted over the low railing, and, clutching the flagpole for support, jabbed with his fist.

He struck a very light, fuzzy body that, somehow, retreated before his blow, and then lunged forward. Hands grabbed him; and he was plummeted back over the railing to the safety of the deck.

The creature followed, striking its wings against the air as it dived at him.

Exactly what instant the searchlight went on, Kenlon had no clear idea. He was fighting, struggling with a human body that was as light as thistledown, but as strong as he was.

Great wings beat down at his head. Abruptly, the birdman broke free.

Kenlon had a flashing glimpse of a lean, intent face, with human lips drawn back to show white teeth. Then the slender body was rising away from him. For a moment, the winged man was silhouetted in the uptilting beam of the searchlight. Then, faster than the shifting light, he spun sideways and was gone into the darkness to the north.

Behind Kenlon, like an anticlimax, a machine gun began to stutter uncertainly into the night.

Chapter 2

Tugging did no good. the shiny pie-plate-like object clung unmoving to the hard steel prow.

Sweating, Kenlon looked up to where Lieutenant Commander Jones-Gordon was kneeling beside the flagpole holding with strong fingers to Kenlon's right wrist while Kenlon worked with his left hand. Trembling from exhaustion, Kenlon finally said:

"What do you think, sir—a blowtorch to burn it off?"

"Who'll wield it?" the commander said drably. "The heat may set off the bomb!"

Incredibly, Kenlon hadn't even thought of it as a bomb. In the excitement, he had forgotten everything but the necessities of the moment.

Now, he felt himself change color. He stared at the object with a horror that presently submerged into the memory that he was a married man with one kid, who had no business getting himself killed.

For a brief moment, that thought held him rigid; then he looked up into Jones-Gordon's eyes. He said with a stiff smile:

"I'm here: I'll do what's necessary."

He raised his voice: "Reichert, bring a blowtorch, and rope scaffolding. Get a couple of men to help. On the double!"

"Aye, aye, sir!"

"It looks transparent; it doesn't look like a bomb," said the commander thoughtfully. He was a square-jawed young man with warm blue eyes. "And besides it's too small to do us any real damage. Come up here, Mr. Kenlon."

Kenlon couldn't have made it himself. Jones-Gordon's strong hands pulled his weakened body over the railing; and only naval training made it possible for him to straighten his trembling form, and stand there rigidly.

His superior said unsmilingly, "It's a good thing I hadn't gone to bed. I wouldn't have believed it if I hadn't seen it myself. Bill, what was it?"

"A man with wings like a bird," Kenlon began.

He stopped. The words jarred through his mind; his whole body grew taut with the unheard-of-reality that was here. He repeated softly:

"A man with wings . . . sir, we must be mad."

Slantwise, out of the corners of his eyes, Kenlon saw the pie tin-shaped "bomb" that the creature had left. And the thought suffered a relapse. If there was madness here, it wasn't of the officers and crew of the *Sea Serpent*. Jones-Gordon was speaking again:

"There are several questions that arise: Where did . . . it . . . come from? What is . . . it? What was its purpose? And where is it now?"

The questions remained unanswered, as Reichert and two men arrived with the required paraphernalia. In a minute Kenlon was dangling from the railing, this time without physical strain.

"It's transparent, all right," he announced, "and the interior looks like an oddly designed radio tube. Get MacRae."

While they waited for the radio operator, Kenlon had time to grasp the eeriness of this scene here in the middle of the Pacific. The glaring searchlight had been shut off. In a darkness broken only by the cautious probings of flashlights, the submarine was like a ghost in an endless black sea.

Now that the marvelous and intricate warship had slowed to a snail's pace, the breeze created by its movement had ceased; and it was hot. Where he was, slung just above the abyss of sea, it seemed even hotter and, as always at night, the area just above water was infinitely blacker.

It was a world apart; somewhere up there in the cloudy

skies, the creature was winging back toward the ship from which it must have come, or perhaps there was no ship.

Kenlon gasped: "Commander, do you realize that there is a possibility the creature has no other point where it can land, *except this submarine?*"

The odd thing was that he had no doubt of it at all now. The birdman would have to come back.

MacRae lowered himself gingerly over the bulging front of the sling on which Kenlon sat. He was a small, chunky man, and he moaned softly to Kenlon:

"If only Mother could see her boy now. But I rise bravely to the emergency, daring all, promising nothing. Hold that flash at an angle, Mr. Kenlon. I'll look in from this side."

Kenlon obliged silently.

"Definitely not a bomb," MacRae grunted. "Electronic, all right, multigrid. Some of the connections don't make much sense." He broke off. "Huh!" he said violently.

"What's the matter?" Kenlon asked quickly.

"There's a little tube inside that's just hanging there in the center of a vacuum. It's not attached to anything. Take a look, Mr. Kenlon, and tell me if I'm crazy. Over to the right. 'Scuse me, that'll be left to you."

Kenlon started to bend down, but before he could get a good look, Lieutenant Commander Jones-Gordon called sharply:

"Mr. MacRae, could that device be used by an enemy submarine to locate us?"

It was a silly question. It didn't sound silly, Kenlon knew that. But it was. It was possible, however, that no one but himself would realize why.

They had only seen the creature flashingly, and from a distance. But he had fought him. He had felt the soft, fuzzy skin; the great *living* wings had hammered at his head. His fingers had clutched a man's slight but powerful body, a body inhumanly light, weighing not more than thirty-five pounds.

Their minds were already growing vague on the details, on the alienness, seeking some natural explanation, something that fitted in with life as it had been lived for ten thousand years, and particularly as it fitted with wars and nations suspicious of each other's weaponry.

But not so long as he lived would he forget the nerve-tingling, the amazing, reality of what he had seen and touched.

And his mind wouldn't reach down to the depths or up to the heights that hid the explanation.

He heard MacRae say: "There's no power source, sir, no battery. I don't see how it can be used for anything as it is now."

The commander must have reached his decision in advance. For he said instantly:

"Both of you come up. Mr. MacRae, you may return below. Mr. Kenlon, I want to talk to you. Paley"—he turned to one of the two assistant machinists—"burn that thing off, but don't let it drop into the sea. We want it. Munson, give Paley a hand."

It was an action taken, a positivity. And it cleared the air. It was a base from which to work. The menace, the sense of alienness, grew dimmer.

When they were alone on the conning tower, Jones-Gordon said grimly:

"Why did he stay? What was his reason for fighting you those few minutes?"

It was not a question to which Kenlon felt he had the correct answer, but he had considered it. He said:

"I think, Commander, he wanted to gain time."

"Time for what?"

"He was fastening that . . . well . . . radio device onto our prow. The solder, or whatever welding process was used, had to be allowed to set."

Jones-Gordon grunted. "Sounds reasonable," he admitted. "He took grave risks."

He added as an afterthought: "We're not through with him yet."

In the darkness, Kenlon stared keenly at his skipper. He had always thought Jones-Gordon a superior business-man type, who had somehow been sidetracked to Annapolis.

His estimate of the officer's capabilities rocketed before this example of adaptability. His earlier opinion, that Jones-Gordon had asked a silly question, had failed to take into account the fact that a commander was required to go to extreme lengths to insure the safety of his ship. And in this particular instance it was also required that he see to it that no other power gained any knowledge of the craft or its performance while it was under his command.

"Have you," Jones-Gordon said, "any suggestions?"

Kenlon shrugged. "We must get that tube off. That's a priority. And I would suggest that the deck patrol carry on all night. It would be a great thing if we could catch him alive. Otherwise"—his lips twisted wryly—"we'd better not even report what we saw."

Lieutenant Commander Jones-Gordon's voice came dryly out of the night: "I see exactly what you mean, Lieutenant. I—"

He broke off, called sharply: "What is it, Munson?"

"Paley asks me to tell you, sir, that the blowtorch won't work on either the thing or the steel around it. Doesn't even get soft, he says. He wants to know what he should do."

It was, Kenlon realized darkly, a fair question.

The night wore on. The *Sea Serpent* had picked up again to cruising speed. The water hissed, the turbines throbbed potently. Kenlon watched anxiously for rifts in the clouds that let the moon come out to stir up the shadows.

But the clouds kept surging back, bringing massed darkness, sometimes reducing visibility to the point where it was almost impossible to see Reichert five feet away as anything but a darker shadow. As for the men pacing the decks . . .

Kenlon groaned. He had no more stomach than Jones-Gordon for turning on the searchlights, but it would have been pleasant to be able to see the *Sea Serpent* in all her gleaming length.

"Mr. Kenlon."

Kenlon jumped, then felt guilty. He hadn't heard the lieutenant commander come through the hatch.

He saluted. "Yes, sir?"

Jones-Gordon came forward and leaned on the railing beside him.

"I've been thinking about your advice, Bill," he said in a low voice, "to dismantle an AA unit and knock that tube off the ship's hide. The answer is no. Here's why."

Kenlon waited, silent.

The other went on: "The *Sea Serpent* is not expendable. Every care must be taken to bring it back to base intact. But what has happened here is unprecedented. *Think* of it—a man that flies with his own wings!" . . . .

Kenlon had been considering that fact for an hour, never quite daring to move all the way on it. He said nothing, but he felt once more that new respect for this commanding officer of his, who had apparently grasped the situation to the extent that he had finally made up his mind about it.

"Bill, I want you to ask yourself—suppose we all took affidavits on this matter on our arrival at base. They'd believe us; I'm sure of that now. Three of the four ranking officers on the new supersub, the pride of the Navy, are not likely to lose their rudders at the same moment."

"Very well, suppose we go back with that plate still attached to our prow, and our story was accepted—do you know what would happen?"

Kenlon had a pretty fair idea. It was a thought that had occurred to him with most of the attendant details during the past hour. He said:

"Scientists would fire on you, as captain, with all their big guns. You would be verbally speared, and held up as a typical sailor without imagination, made stupid by the habit of obedience to *comsubpac*.

"All this, of course, would die down, because the Navy command would come to your defense and say that you had done right to think first of your ship. From time to time, the mystery of the winged man would be taken up in the Sunday supplements, and the action of Lieutenant Commander Jones-Gordon would be deplored. And that *would* be your rank. The Navy would somehow keep passing over you when it came to promotions, on the dimly understood conviction that you had failed a test. Is that picture too strong, sir?"

The other said grimly: "It fits in very neatly with one that I had conjured."

He broke off tautly, "Kenlon, we've got to capture that fellow. I frankly don't see how this can be dangerous. The boys are bringing up some netting, and I'm going to have it arranged so that—"

There was a loud cry from the stern; then a shot; and then the sky above the conning tower darkened. Giant wings made a violent special wind. There was a wild shout from Reichert and a bellow from the lieutenant commander:

"Hold your fire, everybody!"

The next second they had the birdman. It was not an admirable victory. The winged man landed in their midst, and they pounced with a mad abandon. Kenlon twisted one unresisting arm behind the creature's back, and caught at one wing with a desperate will to prevent it from lifting them all into the air.

It didn't even try. The next second, the men with the nets were swarming out of the hatch. The trussing up took about one minute, the lowering through the hatch a little longer, and then . . .

Kenlon was alone with Reichert. He called down to the deck, a little dazedly: "What happened, Johnston? What made you shoot?"

"I found him clinging to the bow, sir."

"You what!" Violently.

"I don't know how long he'd been there, sir."

Taut and cold, Kenlon raced along the deck. His flashlight flared. It was as he had feared. There, attached to the bulging stern, was what looked like an exact duplicate of the "radio" tube on the prow.

Chapter 3

Over the phone, he asked Tedders to call the commander. Jones-Gordon's voice came on the wire a minute later. Kenlon explained what he had discovered. He ended with a quietness that belied his jumping nerves:

"Apparently, sir, he completed his mission against us, and then as there was no other landing place, he surrendered."

There was a silence, then: "I'm sending Mr. Tedders up, Mr. Kenlon. I want you to come down here. Perhaps your command of languages will help us understand what this fellow is trying to say."

It was an eerie scene that Kenlon found. The birdman had been released from the imprisoning nets, and he had had time to smooth his ruffled feathers. He stood at ease in the central supersecret crossfire torpedo room, facing the throng of his captors.

Staring at him, Kenlon briefly forgot everything else. Somehow, all his previous thoughts had been influenced by the night. He had believed himself to be adjusted to this thing.

He wasn't. Here, under the blazing lights, the incredible seemed exactly that.

With an enormous effort, he controlled himself.

The creature man was shorter than he had thought, not more than five feet. His chest looked deformed. It was narrow, and projected like a bird's breastbone. Except for that the body was normal enough, human enough.

Kenlon couldn't see where the wings joined the body, but the wings themselves were in length a little over eight feet each, folded now into two sections, in which position they reached only two feet above the man's head.

The wings were gray, streaked with red and blue. The body was a grayish white, covered with a fine down; the face was white and sensitive looking, with very large eyes.

Kenlon jerked himself out of that detailed examination and turned shakily to Lieutenant Commander Jones-Gordon:

"Sir, what about those two tubes?"

The lieutenant commander stared back steadily. "You know my course, Mr. Kenlon," he said finally, curtly. "However," he added, "I have ordered Mr. Tedders to dismantle an AA deck unit and to destroy *one* of the tubes. We should hear the shots in a few minutes."

It was not absolutely satisfactory. The gun should have been readied earlier as a precaution, even if no immediate action was contemplated. Now that the decision was made delay could mean—well, what could it mean?

In spite of his uncertainty, the conviction came that this was going to be one of the longest waits of his career.

He grew aware that Jones-Gordon had not stopped speaking: ". . . We've already tried seven languages on him; and each time he answers in a tongue that has no resemblance to any of them."

Kenlon did not need to ask what the seven were. Jones-Gordon spoke the halting French and German of the classroom; and there were five national origins among the men: Greek, Polish, Dutch, Russian, and Spanish.

His own German and French would not be needed. Which left only his smattering of Japanese, Cantonese-Chinese, Italian, and Arabic to test.

He started with Japanese. It was his usual lame effort. And the reply it elicited was both startling and depressing.

The answer was dulcetly musical, a very high, sweet tenor, clearly articulated, but sounding in his ears the purest gibberish.

Kenlon wasted no time on his other languages. His watch showed that several minutes had already passed— the three-pounder was due to go off any moment.

He tore out his pencil and notebook, sketched rapidly a

rough design of the submarine, and drew the two tubes in at the points where they had been fastened, with arrows pointing at them.

The birdman took the notebook, glanced at the drawings, and then, with the barest hint of a smile, nodded. The smile was tinged with a curious anxiety, but it disturbed Kenlon more than anything that had yet happened. He had a feeling that the creature was indulging in a sardonic humor.

The impression lasted only a moment. And then the winged man was reaching for the pencil. Kenlon surrendered it, and watched as the man drew swiftly, deftly, on the paper.

It was Jones-Gordon who took the little book when it was finally extended. He frowned at it, then showed it to Kenlon. There were two submarines on the sheet now, and the second one, which had been drawn by the birdman, was a much better replica of the *Sea Serpent* than Kenlon's had been.

In spite of the resemblance, Kenlon's mind jumped stubbornly to the idea that they were advised that there was a second submarine nearby.

It was only after a long moment that he noticed that an open hatch had been added to his sketch, but that the hatch was closed in the birdman's own drawing.

"Sir," he gasped, "he wants us to batten down."

The birdman was reaching for the notebook. The lieutenant commander surrendered it gingerly, and once more the creature sketched rapidly with the pencil.

There was no hint of a smile now on his fine, though rather sharp, features. His face was intent, almost tense, and the drawing was almost flung at the commander, so swiftly was it thrust.

It was a picture of a submarine tilted, and in the act of submerging. The two officers looked at each other. Kenlon said unsteadily:

"I think, sir, I'd better get up on deck and give Tedders a hand."

No word of objection came from Jones-Gordon; and so Kenlon was at the door when the light blazed in his face.

In his face, though in front of him was only the solid steel
door. The light was pouring *through* the door, and
seemed to originate at a distance.

Instantly, it blinked out, but the fantastic thought had
come to Kenlon by the time he reached the hatch:

The tubes! The tubes had lighted; and their intense pal-
pably neutronic glow had poured through four intervening
steel walls. He hadn't seen the second tube at the other
end of the sub but . . .

It didn't matter. Here was the crisis.

Outside, the darkness had lightened. The moon was a
great, pale orb in a widening blue pond of sky. For miles
now, the sea was visible, a black undulating field with
streaks of light showing here and there through the intense velvet.

Against that black, and in that light, the submarine was
a long shape of gleaming metal, making a foaming path in
a sea that heaved and sank, and heaved and sank.

At the forward end of that shining, silvery shape, four
men were engaged in setting up a three-pounder.

That was the facet of the whole vast scene upon which
Kenlon's strained senses fastened.

The gun, the vital gun, was almost ready.

Kenlon sent an uncertain glance back down the hatch.
And felt a little shock of surprise that no one was following him. He hesitated, his mind hard on the sketch the
winged man had drawn.

Hesitation ended. "Quartermaster Reichert," he commanded, "transfer steering to the control room."

"Transfer steering to control. Aye, aye, sir."

Kenlon lowered the hatch into place after Reichert had
gone below and manipulated the electrical locking mechanism. Then he was plunging down to the deck. He
shouted:

"Lieutenant Tedders, fire the instant you are ready.
Fire!"

The flash was red against the uneven sea, the explosion
sharp and loud above the muffled thud of the turbines.

The gun banged metallically as it recoiled and fell over

on the steel deck. The men began to right it, while Tedders poked a flashlight at the "tube."

"Missed!" he groaned.

Kenlon came up. "You didn't miss. I saw the splash of the shell to starboard. It was deflected."

He thought sharply: *Nothing* could be that hard, surely.

He whirled frantically. "Hurry with that gun. I'll fire it this time; and let's try to keep her going. You're sure the shells are nonexploding?"

He didn't wait for the answer. He almost felt the three shells he fired strike. He saw the three splashes far to port. Then the gun fell over. He cried to the men:

"Again! Get it up again!"

To Tedders, he said: "At the very least we'll knock its mechanism out of alignment by concussion. We—"

He had swung with Tedders behind the perspiring, laboring crewmen. And, just like that, they were skeletons, still working there, still standing there.

The light from the tube flowed through them.

But this time it didn't blink off.

Through their bodies, through the gun they were loading, through the intervening projection of the deck, came the glare of the tube.

It was a white glow, so fierce it threatened to burn Kenlon's eyes. Instinctively, he brought up his hand in a self-protecting gesture. He had time to see the bones of his arms and fingers. And then . . .

Then he was struggling, choking, fighting in an appalling depth of warm water.

Chapter 4

Kenlon held his breath. His throat stung from the water he had swallowed. His whole body felt torn by the cataclysm of coughing that threatened to break down the resistance of his clenched muscles.

And all the time he could feel himself rushing upward to the surface. He began to swim frantically, up, up, up. And even in the midst of that prolonged combination of agony and effort, the thought came:

What had happened? What *could* have happened?

Like a shot from a gun he broke the surface, fell back under, then came up clutching for air with his lungs and his hands. His body shook and ached with the wracking labor of his coughs. The water churned as he fought to keep his head above the leaping spray.

He was aware of a mighty roaring of water somewhere in the near distance behind him. Then the thunder subsided, but a series of giant waves smashed him with a sudden violence, swept him along at express speed, and almost engulfed him.

He survived; somehow he survived. The seas became quiet. He disgorged the sickening water he had swallowed, shook the nausea out of his body, and looked palely around him.

A dozen feet away a man's head was bobbing up and down in a rhythm with the choppy beat of the sea. Beyond about a mile distant, was a long, low gray shore, the drab general effect colored here and there with the green of a sparse vegetation.

The shore stretched on, flat and unbroken under a cloud-filled sky, to the horizon on either side.

The whole land scene was strangely, unnaturally repellent in some indescribable way.

Uneasy, Kenlon turned away from it, once more saw the man's bobbing head—and his paralyzed brain came to life.

Tedders? And the men? And the *Sea Serpent?*

The thoughts were like a succession of special pains. With a gasp, Kenlon whirled in the water.

"Dan!" he shrieked. "Dan Tedders!"

A faraway cry answered him. "Here I am, Bill. Here, with Davisson. We're all right. How about you?"

He saw the two heads about three hundred feet to his left. Relieved, Kenlon shouted: "O.K.!"

There were tears in his eyes as he turned once more to the nearby head. Anxiously, he recognized the strained profile of the man.

"Black," he said, "are you all right?"

The man looked dazed. "Yes, sir," he muttered.

Kenlon swam closer. "Are you sure?"

"Yes, sir." Then more wildly: "But my buddy. Johnston, sir! I haven't seen him."

"Johnston!" Kenlon bellowed the words over the water. He twisted, standing up as high as he could, shouted the name again.

There was no answer from that wide and restless sea. Tedders and Davisson were swimming closer. But there was no sign of Johnston.

Thinking back to the agony and the colossal surprise, the miracle was that any of them had survived. He thought: Four out of five! Men were surely strong and wonderful in their determined will to live.

But—where was the *Sea Serpent?*

He wasn't really worried, he told himself shakily. That roaring sound he had heard must have been the sub breaking surface. Any second now she would . . .

There was a long flash of foam in the water two hundred yards seaward. Then a periscope appeared—the *Sea Serpent* swam into size.

As soon as her deck was clear of water, she began to slow. In a few minutes she was riding lightly. Lieutenant

Commander Jones-Gordon was the first to appear. He was followed quickly by half a dozen crew members.

Minutes later, the four men had been dragged aboard. Kenlon reported the loss of Johnston; then, having received permission, went below, and changed his clothes.

As he emerged again from the hatch, Jones-Gordon beckoned him, and said:

"Bill, where are we? What happened?"

It was, Kenlon realized grimly, a sixty-four *hundred* dollar question.

He studied the shore through his glasses, and spent minutes on end peering out over the drab land.

It was an unwholesome vista that unrolled itself as the *Sea Serpent* held to a course parallel to the low-lying beach. The splotches of green showed themselves as nothing but seaweed; and, after an hour, the scene had not changed. After four hours, the shore began to fall away sharply from their course.

It was impossible to be sure whether it was a bay or a permanent direction shift of the shoreline. Kenlon, who had gone to his quarters for a short sleep, climbed up again and watched as the *Sea Serpent* slowed till it was barely creeping along. He turned as Jones-Gordon joined him. The lieutenant commander said:

"I think we'd better lie to, and give our prisoner a going over. I was waiting for you before starting to interview him."

On the way down, the commander added frowningly: "I don't know just what attitude to take toward him. His action is responsible for the death of Johnston, and yet, when you went on deck just before the crisis, he dived over our heads—and prevented us from following you. That precaution on his part undoubtedly saved many lives.

"Similarly," he went on in his precise voice, "in your first struggle with him, he could have knocked you into the sea. Instead, he swept you *up* and back onto the deck.

"Is it possible," the commander continued, "that we should assume that his intentions toward us as individuals are not murderous?"

The question was not of the kind that Kenlon felt qualified to answer. And besides, knowing his superior, he had an idea that the query was purely rhetorical. He tried for a moment to picture the other's intensely practical brain tackling the problem of the winged man and its attendant phenomena.

. It was a strangely hard picture to evoke. He gave it up, conscious, however, that it was not an enviable position for such a man to be in.

They found the winged man industriously sketching in Kenlon's notebook.

"He slept for a while," the guard reported. "When he woke up, he kept pointing to the notebook, so I finally let him have it, sir."

"You did quite right," said the commander. "Just step back now, and keep a sharp watch on us while we're with him."

Kenlon saw, with a thrill of excitement, that the bird-man was beckoning them. It was a strange sensation to step close to that alien form, and bend with—it—over the notebook.

The feeling faded. The notebook and the drawings in it grasped all his attention.

The first page showed an unmistakable sketch of Sol and its first three planets.

The winged man pointed at Earth, then indicated Kenlon and Jones-Gordon with a slender finger. He pointed at Earth again, and this time indicated himself.

Kenlon said, after a silence, "I think he's trying to say, sir, that he is of Earth origin like ourselves."

Jones-Gordon frowned irritably: "Of course he's of Earth. Where else would he be from?"

It struck Kenlon with a pang that this was the flaw he had analyzed in Jones-Gordon, without previously being able to put his mental finger on it.

Abruptly, the skipper's earlier statement that, if he hadn't seen the winged man himself, he wouldn't have believed in him, acquired a new significance. Having seen the impossible, he had accepted it as the fact. He had thus given the illusion of being cognizant of all the implications of the fantastic being who had come into their midst.

He wasn't. His imagination was incapable of grasping the wilder possibilities, the utter normal improbability of such a winged man appearing out of nowhere in mid-twentieth century.

Disappointed, and vaguely disturbed by the unpleasant potentialities, Kenlon did the only logical thing: He held his silence.

"What the devil," said Jones-Gordon, "is this?"

Kenlon emerged from his reverie. His gaze fastened below the drawing of the solar system to a group of figures to which the winged man was pointing:

/
//
///
////
/////
//////

The creature man seemed to realize that he had their attention again, for he pointed at the lone symbol on the top line, then indicated Earth above it, and began slowly to move his finger around the Sun. One, two, three—nine times he made the circuit, and then pointed again at the solitary symbol in the first line of the figures.

Jones-Gordon said curiously: "Is he trying to say that it represents nine years?"

Kenlon said steadily: "I think so, sir."

"Funny way of figuring, if you ask me," the commander grunted. "Why doesn't he make it ten, and simplify the whole problem. What is he doing now?"

The winged man was pointing at the top symbol again. He tapped it with his finger as if he was counting. Kenlon counted with him: one, two, three—eleven. Then the creature man pointed at line two.

"I get it," said Kenlon. "Eleven times nine is ninety-nine. The two symbols stand for ninety-nine years."

A quaver of excitement ran through him. He motioned at the third line.

"If the first two groups are 9 and 99, then the third one must be 11 times 99 or 1089, and so on until—"

He stopped, for the winged man was pointing again at the first figure. He began to tap with his finger. It took a long time this time. A minute passed; and still Kenlon counted on, following the tapping of the finger . . . 90 . . . 100, 101, 102 . . . 111.

The counting ended on 111. Once more the birdman indicated the single symbol, then pointed to the third line.

"Well, 111 times 9," Kenlon said aloud, "equal 999. Which must mean that the fourth line is 1111 times 9 or 9999 years, and so on till the bottom line comes to 999,-999 years. It is an odd way of figuring, but it must have some sound mathematical principle behind it."

He intended to add a comment, but the winged man was rotating his finger rapidly around the Sun. Finally, he picked up the sheet of paper, erased the last two lines and added a second set of four to the fourth line, and then two additional figures. The being now pointed at this line and then at himself.

Kenlon caught his breath in amazement. What was the creature saying? *What* was he trying to say?

He grabbed at the sheet and stared at it. It showed:

/
//
///
//// //// //

"Twenty-five thousand years," Kenlon heard himself say in a flat voice. "I think he's trying to tell us that we've been brought twenty-five thousand years into the future."

After a dazed moment, Kenlon saw that there was a look of exasperation on Jones-Gordon's face. The lieutenant commander made a gesture of irritation. "It's evident," he said, "that we're getting nowhere in this attempt at communication. What's on the next page?"

Without a word, Kenlon turned the page. The sheet

showed a sketch of a submarine heading for an object floating in the sky above the sea. He studied it, puzzled. After a blank moment, he decided it was a mountain rising out of the sea.

The only thing was, it was unmistakably drawn as being above the sea, comletely unattached.

Kenlon decided to ignore that. He concentrated on the mountain. It rose sheer on every visible side, and the crown was capped by an enormous building. Dozens of winged men were flying around the massive structure. Others were standing in openings carved high in the towering building. Still others were hovering just above the water, fighting something that was trying to come up from the sea.

It was strange, that sense of them fighting something. But it was unmistakable. Yet there seemed only to be men in the water.

With a deliberate effort, Jenlon pulled his mind away from the examination. He caught the keen, hawklike eyes of the winged man, pointed at the mountain, then indicated various directions. He hoped that there would be no question about what he was asking.

There wasn't. The sharp face grew excited, smiling, eager. A wing fluttered, and half-pointed with one arm away from the land and from the course the *Sea Serpent* had been pursuing.

Jones-Gordon's voice broke the silence. "Now that," he said, "is impossible. How can he tell from inside the boat here what direction we should follow? He can't possibly know whether or not we changed course while he was sleeping."

Kenlon hesitated. It struck him that his own imagination might be considered irresponsible because of the way he had jumped at conclusion after conclusion on the basis of flimsy evidence. A suggestion that the winged man's sense of direction was possibly related to the instincts of a homing pigeon might be the straw that would break the camel's back.

Nevertheless, he had always felt that an officer should

express his opinions when asked. That should apply particularly under unusual circumstances.

Still he hesitated. And finally it seemed to him that Lieutenant Commander Jones-Gordon's mind had been strained enough for the moment. He grew aware that the skipper was speaking:

"You're the linguist in our outfit, Lieutenant. I want you in your spare time to learn his language and teach him ours. But first—come on deck."

Kenlon followed reluctantly. His whole being seemed to palpitate in his desire to begin establishing communication with the winged man. But he waited quietly, as Jones-Gordon stood for several minutes staring at the shore. The commander said abruptly:

"We can't go blindly on along this strange shore in shallow and unknown waters.

"Since the clouds haven't cleared for a moment, it's impossible to tell what time of day it is; so I've decided that we'll stay here overnight and"—he turned to Kenlon, finished briskly—"in the morning you will head an expedition into the interior, remaining several days if necessary, but try to find out everything possible."

Chapter 5

Kenlon began to feel excited.

It wasn't the shore of itself. That remained unprepossessing, repellent, exactly as when he had first seen it. Gray and flat it spread before him, nearer and nearer as the motorboat sputtered toward it.

He could see inland about a mile. Beyond that the gray of the sky and the gray of the land blurred further vision.

It didn't matter. In an hour they would have penetrated out of sight of the sea, unless this was a long, narrow island, in which even the water would be there on the other side, restlessly awaiting them.

Jones-Gordon had offered the theory that it was an island, adding with an uneasy attempt at logic:

"The Pacific is probably the only body of water that has never been thoroughly explored. There are possibly scores of small atolls that have never been recorded on any map."

Kenlon had pricked that little bubble brutally:

"We followed the shore of this *small*, undiscovered island for four hours at twenty-four knots. And just how did we get opposite it so suddenly and from night into day?"

The instant he had spoken he regretted it. There was no point in fighting a man's basic character. Nevertheless, for a moment his irritation at an intelligent human being who reacted to a winged man much as he would have acted if he had seen an ordinary South Sea native under similar provocative conditions, was—well, infuriating.

Out of the corner of his eyes, Kenlon saw one of Gainishaw's hands leave the wheel, and reach toward him.

"Mr. Kenlon," the helmsman gasped. "What's that over there? Looks like a man swimming. He's watching us."

"Huh!" said Kenlon. His mind leaped to thought of Johnston. He jumped to his feet with a low cry. One look verified that it wasn't Johnston. It was—what?

Kenlon blinked incredulously, and stared at the largest human being he had ever seen. The man was plainly visible not more than a hundred feet away, almost directly in the path of the motorboat. He was at least eight feet in length, and he had very big eyes. He was swimming toward the left parallel to the shore with an easy overhand motion, and he was naked.

His speed was even greater than it seemed. In following him, the motorboat had to turn at full right angles to its course. Just before they drew up to him, the swimmer turned in the water like an animal at bay.

It was a strong, beefy but intelligent countenance that faced up to them. The man's ears, Kenlon observed, were very flat against his head; his nose was small, almost stubby and, upturned as it was, revealed only the barest suggestion of nostrils. The mouth, however, was normal with sturdy, white teeth.

The swimmer's large eyes stared at the boat and its occupants with a keen, absorbed appraisal, but utterly without fear.

"Careful!" Kenlon cautioned. "Steer clear of him. Don't let him grab the gunwale. *Watch out!*"

But the boat had slowed too much. Its propeller reversed, it was not maneuverable. Before the forward impulse could be resumed, before the motor could even speed up, the strange giant had lunged toward the boat. Thick fingers clutched the gunwale—and he was aboard.

It was the fastest, strongest movement Kenlon had ever seen. With a hiss of indrawn breath, he snatched his gun from his holster; and then, seeing that the monster was making no threatening movement, held his fire.

The motorboat ceased its wild swaying; and Kenlon saw that only one man had succeeded in getting his rifle into firing position. Kenlon yelled warningly:

"Hold your fire, Pannatt."

The stranger had been standing with back toward Kenlon. At the sound of Kenlon's voice, he half-turned; then he seemed to think better of it. He stepped forward, toward Gainishaw at the wheel. And once more changed his mind.

Like a streak, he whirled, and snatched the gun from Pannatt's fingers. The instant he had the gun, his manner changed again. An unmistakable aura of curiosity exuded from the very attitude of his body.

It was so completely lacking in hostility that Kenlon, on the verge of pressing the trigger, relaxed his finger, and waited.

He was astounded. He felt himself in the presence of a man who was his superior in every way; a man so quick, mentally and physically, that actions which would have resulted in the death of ordinary men, left him untouched, not even threatened.

It was all too swift. The vagrant thought came to Kenlon: Should he capture this man? Before he could even think about it, the giant had solved the mechanism of the Garand.

He fired the gun into the water; and then, as if instantly realizing all its implications, assumed an attitude of contempt. Without a word, exuding derision, he handed the weapon back to Pannatt. Then he was at the wheel.

He seemed to know where the engine would be; or perhaps he had noted that before. Up came the doors, and he was bending over the motors, curious, absorbed, intent. For a moment, Kenlon saw only the massive legs, the more massive buttocks.

The moment gave him time to think: "Grab him!" he said softly. And dived forward.

He was not roughly handled. The giant twisted about, and caught him with a strength that brooked no resistance—and held him up for one of those lightning examinations.

For the first time, Kenlon saw the creature's front. It was such a fleeting glance that he had only time to notice that the other seemed to be wearing something frilly on his dark brown chest, partly under the great arms.

The next instant he had been set down; and there was a splash. Kenlon stood dumb and useless trying to force his mind to think of what he had seen.

Not gills, he thought; it couldn't have been gills. There was no way of verifying. Though they waited ten minutes, the human fish did not reappear.

He decided against returning to the ship. The episode must have been observed; and he could send a brief report back to the skipper with Gainishaw. After he had scrawled his account, he decided to put the affair out of his mind. Later, he would think it over.

But the thought did come that *this* was what the birdman must have been fighting in the water at the foot of their mountain eyrie.

He turned his attention to the shore, which was very near now. He said to Gainishaw:

"Careful. I imagine there's a very gradual falling off of the land into water. Let's see how far we can go."

Surprisingly, they made it to within fifteen feet of shore before the nose of the motorboat sank gently into the black ooze.

Kenlon said: "O. K., I guess we'll have to walk. Rifer, Smiley, Glabe, Ridell, Pannatt—your packs and your guns! Let's go!"

Two of the men jumped for shallow water. Kenlon lowered himself over the side with some attempt at dignity.

His feet touched the mud, and kept right on going. He saw with a blank horror the two men who had jumped sink like stones into a bottomless mud. Two appalled screams rent the air, then a horrid gurgling—and silence except for the mutter of the throttled motor.

He was struggling, fighting. The weight of his pack—fifty pounds—helped the clutching mud. But his fingers were still holding onto the gunwale. And they didn't let go.

He drew himself up. The boat rocked; and there was a sound of other men panting and wheezing with effort; and then one of Gainishaw's hands closed over his right wrist, and the other caught the collar of his shirt.

The mud released him with a faint squitch. He splashed with his feet. Then he fell into the bottom of the boat. For a moment, he lay there empty-minded; then all his consciousness poured back, and he scrambled to his knees in time to give Smiley a hand up while Gainishaw pulled Glabe and Ridell into the boat.

While the rescued men drooped with exhaustion, Kenlon snatched a canvas from the tool chest, and tossed it onto the shore opposite them. He whirled.

"Back to the ship!" he commanded. "Top speed. We've got to make some attempt to rescue Pannatt and Rifer."

He pictured the two men, held in suspension beneath the mud, their lungs full of water they had swallowed before the mud sucked them under.

For the next half hour, they might still be rescuable.

Jones-Gordon came back with them. In a rubber dinghy, then, sweating men hovered over the mud with hooked sticks, and probed for bodies.

After three minutes they pulled up Rifer, a gray, limp mass. The skipper and Kenlon worked over him alternatively, then sent him back to the *Sea Serpent*. Jones-Gordon went aboard to carry on with the resuscitation; Kenlon returned to where the dinghy was dragging the mud.

In about fifteen minutes the signal was flashed from the conning tower that Rifer had come to. Briefly, that enlivened the search. But after an hour there was still no sign of Pannatt.

Kenlon remembered the man, a wiry little Iowan, with cheerful gray eyes, and a habit of doing everything on the double. Not married! Which was something. One of the nightmares of the service was composing letters to the widows of the deceased.

But even that had its other side. There was something inexpressibly tragic about a man who had no home, no friends except a few shipmates like himself, going into the oblivion of a bottomless world of mud. Terrible that there were so many men on these ships whom no one would remember beyond a few days. Kenlon grew aware that Gainishaw was trying to attract his attention.

"The skipper, sir, is signaling for the motorboat to return."

"Very well," Kenlon nodded.

There was no doubt that it was time to call off the search, but the prospect depressed him. To his surprise, Jones-Gordon climbed in with him, and they returned to the scene of the disaster.

The lieutenant commander explained: "The men wouldn't like it if I did not personally supervise the final steps. Even if we found Pannatt now, we could only give him a sea burial. You agree with that, don't you?"

Kenlon agreed; and the other man went on: "What do you make of this mud, Bill?"

Kenlon shook his head. "I never saw anything like it, sir. The particles were so fine that they don't even form a crust." He motioned toward the land. "All the top layer is dry. It looks hard, and yet the individual particles do not cling together to form a cohesive mud pack. Perhaps we should test it further along the shore. It seems incredible there isn't any dry land at all."

Jones-Gordon scowled decisively. "Put me back on the *Sea Serpent* and make the tests," he commanded.

In spite of the earlier words, Kenlon felt a shock. "Rescue operations suspended?" he asked.

The skipper nodded. "Suspended."

It was one thing to cease physical operations, quite another to suspend them mentally. As they pushed cautiously along the shore, probing that deceiving and murderous land, Kenlon kept seeing the man sinking down, down into the depths of an eight-thousand-mile in diameter ball of mud.

He thought: What was the matter with him? After all, he had seen death before. It must be the manner of the death—and the setting.

The setting! Was it possible they were actually 24,999 years into the future? And *this* gray horror was the destiny of the continents?

His mind reverted to thought of the swimming giant

and the winged man. After a moment it was clear that for the *Sea Serpent* and its officers and men what had happened was but the beginning.

There seemed no conceivable satisfactory ending.

Chapter 6

Kenlon found it a hard language to learn, and the bird-man had the same difficulty with English. Ordinary words like hand, foot, wing, when the creature pronounced them, were almost incomprehensible. And Kenlon's efforts to imitate the melodic sounds of the winged man only made his tutor shake his head sadly.

As Kenlon made it out, the winged being pronounced *r* like *a* in father, except that the sound contained the barest hint of the consonant hardness. A similar difficulty obtained with fully half of the other letters.

Kenlon saw, however, that their anxiety, their sense of urgency, was about equal, and, by the end of the fourth week, they could write each other's languages with fair ease, though speech remained a laborious process.

On the thirty-first day, he felt sure enough of himself to bring Jones-Gordon down to interview the prisoner. For a whole week, on the basis of the flimsy vocabulary he had picked up from the birdman, and influenced by the messages the creature had persistently tried to put over both in his speaking and his writing, he had been jotting down questions.

He had divided the questions into two sections. He handed over the first section, and then sat watching the strained face of the birdman, while the man wrote, as they had agreed, the answer to each question, first in English, then in, well, whatever it was.

After four weeks, Kenlon thought, as he waited. For a whole month, the *Sea Serpent* had lain motionless in a choppy gray sea beneath a perpetually clouded sky a mile from a terrible land that wasn't land at all.

It was a ship of badly frightened, bewildered men. Funny, that fright. Some of the men aboard had grinned their way through World War II, in spite of the knowledge that at any moment depth bombs might start exploding. Now they looked haunted and fearful in the face of a danger of unplumbed dimensions.

And there was nothing they could do, nothing that could be done for them. Jones-Gordon, the practical, had lost ten pounds, and the reality must have sunk deep indeed into him because not once during the entire month did the ship move.

Especially significant of the change that time had wrought was that Jones-Gordon had read Kenlon's proposed questions and approved them without comment.

They sat and waited. Kenlon caught himself surreptitiously watching, not the winged man, but Lieutenant Commander Jones-Gordon. The commander's face was impassive, though there were vaguely anxious lines around his eyes.

Sitting there, studying that rather heavy, strong but unimaginative, earnest, brave countenance, Kenlon had the sudden conviction that, no matter what mental concessions the other was prepared to make to reality, the situation would still always be too big for him.

Not, Kenlon thought wryly, that he himself was equipped except for his curious *willingness* to adapt himself, to handle what was here.

The birdman's voice trilled across Kenlon's reverie: "Heaa you aaa."

Jones-Gordon jumped. Kenlon made no effort to take the notebook extended by the winged man, but silently indicated the skipper. Rather reluctantly, the winged man handed it over.

The lieutenant commander began to read. It didn't take long. When he had finished, he sat for a while seemingly lost in thought; abruptly, he handed the note sheet to Kenlon, who read:

Q. Is this Earth?
A. Yes.

Q. Is it Earth of our future?
A. Yes.
Q. How far in our future?
A. A.D. 24,999.
Q. Are we in the same ocean?
A. Yes.
Q. How many oceans are there on Earth now?
A. Three big lands. The rest is ocean.
Q. How many lands?
A. See above.
Q. Why is the land so soft?
A. It suddenly became soft. Nobody knows why.
Q. How long ago did this disaster happen?
A. 3999 years ago.
Q. Is there any hard land?
A. Only our island in the sky.
Q. What is your name?
A. Nemmo.

Kenlon did not look up immediately. None of the answers given was new to him. But he wondered if he should discuss them as if they were or quite frankly admit that he had known it for some time. Until this instant he had thought that the moment would decide the problem. Now that the moment was here, the decision still rested squarely with him.

He sighed. Still undecided, he handed the rest of the questions to Nemmo, waited until the winged man had bent to his labored answering, and then turned to Jones-Gordon and said cautiously:

"I gathered some of this stuff from what—Nemmo—has written to me from time to time in doing his exercises in English. My questions, as you can see by their pointedness were partly based on that advance knowledge."

He paused, giving his chief time to say something, if he desired to. The pause was also designed to give himself a further chance to decide on how far he should admit familiarity with the facts. No comment came from the skipper, and after a minute Kenlon went on swiftly but carefully:

"There's not much can be said. The answers either speak for themselves, or we are all mad. One curious fact is the numer system. Instead of saying approximately 25,-000 years, Nemmo says, 24,999. It looks awkward, but it is already apparent that winged men use nine as we use zero.

"In its way, that is a devastatingly convincing point. It's strange, genuinely alien in concept, and yet oddly logical. Nine, if you think about it, is almost as wonderful a number as ten. Perhaps *they* found it more so. Perhaps they have discovered mathematical uses for it of which we have no knowledge.

"I'm not going to press this point. At the moment, all I know about the number nine is that it can be used to verify the answers of problems in addition, subtraction, multiplication, and division."

Once more Kenlon paused. This time he stole a look at the skipper. The lieutenant commander was sitting stiffly, his eyes staring fixedly straight ahead. After a moment, there seemed nothing to do but speak further. Kenlon did so reluctantly:

"It's very possible that, after four thousand years, these winged men don't really know what happened. Perhaps, the polar caps melted and raised the world's water level. Certainly, there has to be an explanation of why we arrived in this era in such a depth of water. My personal impression is that I came up through at least a hundred feet of water before I broke surface. As for Nemmo's statement that the home of the flying men actually floats in the sky above the sea—"

Jones-Gordon stirred. His face muscles rippled, enlivening his tanned skin. He said in an expressionless voice, "I think, Mr. Kenlon, we had better see the rest of the answers before we go deeper into interpretations."

It was as bluntly worded an invitation to silence as Kenlon had ever received from Jones-Gordon. He did not let it worry him. What was disturbing was the evidence it gave of the lieutenant commander's state of mind. His words left no doubt that the practical brain was reeling.

At last the winged man looked up. "Fidished!" he said. He thereupon handed the skipper the question-and-answer sheets. Jones-Gordon read them, then passed them on to Kenlon.

Q. Are there more winged men?
A. Approximately 239,999.
Q. Where do they live?
A. On our metal island in the sky.
Q. What are they called?
A. Men.
Q. How can we get to them?
A. I will point the way. I want you and the ship to go there.
Q. How did your people learn to fly?
A. We were made. Men of the ground like yourself saw that the mud could not be stopped. There was nowhere to escape to. So they made some men for flying, and some for swimming. They were wonderful, those groundmen. They knew everything. But they are all dead now. A great tragedy.
Q. Why do you weigh so little?
A. My bones are hollow; my flesh light and strong. I have been eating your foods sparingly, because they are too heavy. There are extra lungs inside my bones.
.Q Are there other men on Earth?
A. Some were made by the groundmen for swimming. These people are our enemies. They live in a metal island under water. They hate us and intend to destroy us. We brought you here to demolish their city under the sea.
Q. Why did you bring us here?
A. You must destroy the metal city of the fishermen.
Q. Can you put us back to our time?
A. We will put you back when you have destroyed the city of our enemy.

The turbines began their steady murmur. The three-hundred-fifty foot steel machine ceased its rolling, turned slowly onto its new course, and began to pick up speed. In half an hour, the flat, gray land was completely merged with the gray waters and the gray sky.

Kenlon turned as Jones-Gordon joined him at the railing. The lieutenant commander said:

"I thought you might like to know my reasons for setting our course for this eyrie of the winged men, if there is such a place."

Kenlon nodded, but said nothing. The skipper stood frowning for a moment, then resumed abruptly:

"First of all, if this fantastic place of theirs is actually floating in the sky somewhere ahead, its existence will provide verification for the rest of the story."

Kenlon nodded again, again said nothing. The thought came to him, however, that an intelligent man who needed further evidence that they were not in the twentieth century, wherever else they might be, was a—he couldn't decide exactly what.

It was possible, of course, that so unimaginative a human being, a man whose mind was solidly attached to the realities he knew, might be very useful in keeping them all down to earth in a stabilizing sense of the phrase.

Might! Kenlon's brow crinkled ever so slightly. There were other potentialities that were not so attractive.

"The second reason," Jones-Gordon went on, "why it is desirable to visit the island is because *there* will be located the time machine responsible for bringing the *Sea Serpent* to *this*."

He waved his hand at the now limitless ocean and made a wry face.

"Thirdly," he continued coolly, "the fact that they have found it necessary to search through time for a war machine that will serve their purpose of underwater destruction suggests that this submarine is the greatest weapon now existing in the year of 24,999 A.D."

Jones-Gordon looked sharply at Kenlon. "Do you agree with that?"

Kenlon hesitated. It was a good point; he had to admit that. He said slowly:

"At least, their defenses are good. A three-pound shell didn't even dent the metal used in the construction of their electronic time tube. Of course, Nemmo told me, when I was questioning him about the tube, that the groundmen used a uniformly thick metal in all their general purpose work. I venture to say that, strong as it is, it couldn't stand up against one of our torpedoes."

Jones-Gordon was nodding with savage satisfaction. "We have aboard, Mr. Kenlon, forty-eight of the mightiest explosive weapons of our age. I think we can dominate any situation."

Kenlon shook his head. "People who can build a time machine, sir, are not to be discounted. To my mind, the weakness of these birdmen is not intelligence, but materials. They probably have no mining facilities, nothing but their home.

"I suggest that the same limitation has not applied to the fishmen, which is why they are dangerous to the birdmen. I cannot emphasize too strongly that the specimen we saw was superhuman in every sense of the word. He was—"

Kenlon paused, amazed at the awe that abruptly affected his voice, and flowed like fire through his body. He shook himself, finished rather weakly:

"The winged men lack the equipment to reach the fishmen, but the reverse situation does not obtain."

There was no immediate answer. Jones-Gordon stood staring out to sea, his heavy face almost expressionless. Kenlon recognized the fatalistic look that finally came into the lieutenant commander's eyes. The officer said in a curiously quiet voice:

"If our situation is as this creature described, then we are, so far as the United States Navy is concerned, an expended unit. By that statement you will see that I take no stock in their promise to return us to our own time when we have accomplished this ridiculous purpose of theirs. I think we are justified in assuming that we are lost men and are, therefore, free of all constraint and all the petty alarms of men who still retain hope."

He stopped; and Kenlon sighed inwardly. Like all human beings, Jones-Gordon could not be docketed into one pigeonhole. Practical he might be, but in this mood his character changed almost completely. Somehow, long ago, the lieutenant commander had resigned himself to death. It had made him fearless, cool, and unexcitable in battle, the perfect commander.

It was theoretically possible that all the men who went down to the sea in submarines should similarly surrender themselves to a fatalistic acceptance of death. But they hadn't. Kenlon hadn't. In battle, his nerves had tensed to violin-string tautness. His mind was as cold as the metal plates of the sub in which he served; his calmness was the artificial calm of the trained man who has a job to do and does it.

But he feared death. Sometimes at night he would wake up sweating from a dream in which they had been sunk, and the water was pouring in with a hellishly final violence. He said now:

"Then you have no intention of doing as the winged men desire?"

The answer was cool, and devastating in its logic:

"The United States Navy does not engage in private wars, regardless of inducement. It obeys orders and defends itself when attacked.

"There is only one group here that can be said to have attacked us. We—"

There was a shout: "Land ho! Straight ahead, sir."

One glance was all that Kenlon needed. They had come to the island in the sky.

To the naked eye it showed as a vague shape rising up apparently out of the sea, its upper reaches lost in the clouds above. It was not until he looked through his glass that Kenlon saw that the—mountain—was at least fifty, possibly seventy-five, miles away.

Its shape was roughly as Nemmo had drawn it that first day, except that the walls did not seem quite so sheer, were, in fact, distinctly triangular, angled up to provide a base for the building which was still almost completely buried in the perpetual nimbostratus clouds.

Far ahead of the submarine, it began to rain. The mountain was blotted out. When the rain ended after more than an hour, Kenlon shed his oils and watched as the eyrie of the winged men once more showed through the mist.

It was still in the distance, but the rift between its base and the sea was plainly visible at last through his glass. He could make out too, more clearly now, the building that crowned the dark mountain. But nothing else. Distance hid whatever signs of life were manifesting on the enormous black triangle of sky island. The deadness, the alienness, the *impossibility* of what he was seeing enormously intensified the anxiety that had been gathering in Kenlon.

It was time, he thought grimly, that he forgot his semi-friendliness toward the winged men, product of his month's close associaiton with the quiet and gentle Nemmo, and remember that a United States submarine had been brought forcibly into a strange world on an "or else" basis.

What was needed here was the cold objectivity and devotion to duty of a Jones-Gordon, and no weakness at all. And yet . . .

Undecided, he raised his glass again, examining the base of the mountain. From his low vantage point, he was not able to see the water underneath, but there were several shapes there that seemed to be lying in the water, one of them a torpedolike structure so long and sinister looking that Kenlon felt a chill along his spine.

He hesitated. The lieutenant commander was sleeping; and on this, as on all submarines, the command centered so peculiarly around the skipper that Kenlon had long since formed the habit of leaving all basic decisions to Jones-Gordon.

He shook himself. They were in dangerous water; and that was reason enough to prepare the ship. He called sharply:

"You men down there on deck—get below."

They came, scrambling. Kenlon phoned the diving officer:

"Mr. Gagnon, open the Kingston valves in the fore and aft main ballast tanks."

"Open the Kingston valves fore and aft. Aye, aye, sir."

There was a swirling sound as water rushed into the tanks. The *Sea Serpent* settled perceptibly, and slowed as her decks were washed by the rising sea. The water lashed up to the base of the conning tower, then rose no more. The sound of the water pouring into the tanks yielded to the pressure of the air that was still in the tanks, and ceased. Riding on her vents, rigged for diving within seconds, the *Sea Serpent* slid on through the gray ocean. The readjustment had barely been completed when Jones-Gordon climbed onto the bridge.

"I was hoping, sir," Kenlon greeted him, "you wouldn't be awakened by the sound of the water. It was a precaution only."

He explained about the objects in the water below the eyrie, finished:

"They're harder to see now that we'er running awash, but they're still visible."

For a long minute Jones-Gordon stood staring through his glass. He turned finally. "Go below and ask our prisoner what they could be."

Nemmo frowned over Kenlon's written question. His wings fluttered abruptly in a way that Kenlon had observed indicated excitement. He wrote:

"Others like myself were sent into various periods of time. Apparently some of these were successful in bringing back warcraft from other ages than your own. There is no historical record, however, of submarines being used after the twentieth century except for undersea exploration. And only a submarine, it seems to me, could be successful against the city of the swimming men."

Chapter 7

An hour later, as they hove-to within a mile of the large vessel, Kenlon studied the craft. It was not less than a thousand feet in length, and it was all metal. There were other smaller ships lying on the water. Kenlon, facing port, was anxiously scanning these through his glass, when he heard a faint splash.

He turned and saw the two giants. "Watch out!" he yelled.

He snatched his gun and leaped toward Jones-Gordon. Incredibly, he was too late. Before the lieutenant commander could back away from the railing, the great hands had him. He was lifted, actually torn from his position, so swift was it all. A monstrous splash, the gurgling of a man drowning, and a trail of bubbles! Kenlon saw the three bodies for a brief moment twenty feet beneath the surface. Then there was a flick of flesh color, and they were gone into the depths.

Not until then, when it was immeasurably too late, did he fire his gun. The four shots and the accompanying splashes echoed futilely on the humid air. There was silence except for the restless swishing of the sea. The motors had stopped. The submarine rolled uneasily in the sullen waters under the overhanging mountain that floated in the sky above them.

The silence ended. "Merciful heavens!" gasped the helmsman five feet from where Kenlon stood staring into the dark sea.

The words broke the spell. The paralysis drained from Kenlon. He poised there a moment longer still weak from reaction, and then, abruptly conscious that everything now depended on him, he came to full life.

His first desperate impulse was to take the sub down in pursuit of the murderers. Instantly he realized that he couldn't do anything so hopelessly foolish. He stood very still, forcing himself to think, to feel, to let the realities sink into him: the faint sounds, the salty, tangy smell of the sea, the alien facts of the visible life around him—all these his body and mind soaked up like an insatiable sponge. And finally the esscence of all that extrania was integrated. The first series of answers came, and he knew the action that he must take.

Rescue was impossible, but one thing was certain: Over a reasonably long given course, the *Sea Serpent* could outdistance any fish, human or otherwise, in the wide gray ocean. Therefore he could get to the city of the fishmen ahead of the murderers. Whatever purpose they had with the skipper's body could be frustrated by getting there first and waiting for them.

Kenlon snatched the phone out of its waterproof box and called the engine room. "Half speed ahead, both engines, Mr. Craig."

"Half speed ahead, both engines. Aye, aye, sir."

The turbines hissed. The *Sea Serpent* began to move. Kenlon turned to the helmsman. "Durosky, set a circular course around that very large vessel over there, keeping at about this distance. Run her around and around until further notice."

The terrible taut feeling began to lift from Kenlon. The consciousness that Jones-Gordon was dead was a constriction around his heart, but his brain and body were functioning now, and, as always in the past, the iron demands of duty eased the shock and the pain.

The *Sea Serpent* was moving. No fishman could now hope to keep pace with her, let alone scramble aboard. There was time to carry out the next necessary step toward his goal. But first . . .

Once more, Kenlon used the phone. This time he called Tedders.

"Rouse Benny, Dan," he said grimly, "and bring him up to the bridge without delay."

"Where's the skipper?" asked the irrepressible Tedders, as he came through the hatch. "I thought he was up here. And what about the shots that were fired?"

The expression on Kenlon's face must have struck him then, for his eyes widened, and he stared wildly at the bleak, fantastic scene.

Kenlon waited until Lieutenant Benjamin had climbed onto the bridge. The second officer looked around swiftly. His gaze took in the overhanging eyrie, narrowed speculatively on the torpedo-shaped machine; then flicked back to Kenton. He saluted and stood expectant. Kenlon began:

"Durosky!"

The helmsman saluted. "Aye, aye, sir!"

"Tell Mr. Benjamin and Mr. Tedders what you saw happen to the skipper. And all of you remain on fullest alert. I am going below to get a course from Nemmo."

He plunged down the hatch. Nemmo looked up in surprise from a copy of the *Times* he was bending over in his intent way.

Kenlon didn't pause to write his question. He made his request verbally in the language of the winged men, and he must have been understood, for Nemmo looked at him sharply—and refused to give the information.

"I'm sorry," he said in English. "From your agitation I can see that something has happened. But my duty was to bring you to the vicinity of our city. In a few minutes one of my fellows will undoubtedly establish contact with you.

"For some reason, our council warned us against giving this information until it gives the signal. And we must follow its advice. If for any reason we change our minds, I shall let you know."

Minutes later, he had still not changed that attitude.

Kenlon forced calm upon his jumping nerves. He stood finally, chewing his lip, letting the tension drain from his body. He felt almost ill from the excitement, first from reaction to what had happened, then from the developing feverishness of his effort to obtain from Nemmo a directive concerning the location of the city of the fishmen. It wasn't, he told himself, that great speed was absolutely necessary. He had the impression somehow that the fish-men lived a considerable distance away. The *Sea Serpent* could make thirty knots on the surface, and, therefore. provided there was not too much delay, could easily get to the city ahead of the two murderers and the body they were transporting.

A small depth charge expelled from a torpedo tube would do the rest.

He grew aware that Nemmo was speaking again. "What has happened?" the winged man asked.

Kenlon hesitated. His reasons for withholding until now the fact of the skipper's death were varied. They were partly rooted in Jones-Gordon's logic that the winged men were enemies, a dictum with which Kenlon disagreed, but which, as dutiful officer, he had not questioned. In the second place he had not wanted to give these flying folk the idea that the officers and crew of the *Sea Serpent* were now automatically on their side.

As the lieutenant commander had said, the United States Navy did not fight private wars.

Nevertheless, the fishmen must want the body for some purpose, or they wouldn't have taken it with them. The winged men might know what that purpose would be. With abrupt decision, Kenlon described the attack. When he had finished, Nemmo stared at him with troubled eyes.

"I have no idea," he said finally, with a curious precision, "what they would do with a dead body." He paused, finished: "And what is your plan?"

Kenlon explained that, too. For a long moment, then, the winged man was silent. At last he said:

"And what are you going to do with me—keep me aboard, or release me?"

It was a complete change of subject, and Kenlon smiled with a wry sense of defeat as he considered the vain possibility that Nemmo might be persuaded to change his mind. His close association with the man had given him an impression of an honest, scholarly man with a negative personality. Nemmo had seemed much more alive when they had first captured him. But that was probably due to their intense awareness of his wings, his alienness.

There could be no doubt, however, of the winged man's strength of will. A man who could take the risks he had taken in going into the distant past, wouldn't weaken now if he had decided not to tell something.

But Kenlon's purpose remained too strong for him to accept any kind of refusal. He ignored the other's question, said quickly:

"Will you answer this: How far are we from the city of the fishmen?"

The words must have contained his first big phonetic error, because Nemmo seemed not to understand. The hindrance jarred Kenlon into startled realization: for minutes on end now, they had been talking together with only occasional hesitations. He said wonderingly:

"You know, Nemmo, under stress we don't do too badly with these new languages." He paused, frowning. "Well, why shouldn't we? We had three hundred hours of sustained study without interference from other students. That's almost as much time as I gave to German and French."

He caught himself, remembering his purpose, and repeated his question, with emphasis this time. "How far . . . from their city?"

Once more, the winged man sat pondering as if he was considering angles to the problem, of which Kenlon knew nothing. At last, he shook his head gravely.

"Lieutenant, if I had my way, I would gladly give you this information. The fact, however, that not even now are you ready to attack the sea city is disturbing. But there is the council. It has barred the transmission of knowledge relating to the location of the city under the sea. The bar, as I said before, troubles all the winged men, but we are not resisting the council's decisions."

He picked up the copy of the *Times* that he had been reading, then added:

"One precaution! The moment a member of my race arrives, tell him the gihlander protective lamps should be adjusted before your ship comes to rest."

Kenlon did not answer. He felt exhausted as if he had strained too hard against a heavy object. He made his way toward the hatch, but paused to gulp down a cup of coffee and a doughnut. A seaman came running.

"Mr. Kenlon, sir. Mr. Benjamin says to tell you that a flying boat has put off from one of the other ships and is coming toward us."

Kenlon reached the deck in thirty seconds flat.

Chapter 8

The scene outside was much the same as when he had left it, except that everything was from a different angle. The *Sea Serpent's* circular course had taken her to the far side of the big ship. Near and shiny red in color was the second largest vessel, a narrow, high-decked craft with a transparent hood over her entire length. And it was from her, apparently, that the flying boat had come.

The machine was coming very slowly, not less than three but not more than five knots an hour. Her line of approach would take her across the *Sea Serpent's* course approximately a mile farther on. Kenlon could already make out human figures sitting in her.

The sight stirred an emotion deep in his mind. A consciousness came of the wonder of this moment, of the tremendous and exciting events that were transpiring minute by minute.

But the violent death of Jones-Gordon was too recent. The stirring, the thrill, ceased. His interest declined. Bleakly, he turned toward the two officers. He said in a colorless voice:

"Durosky has told you about the skipper?"

They nodded. Both men were white. Benjamin saluted, said:

"You may count on our loyalty, sir."

Dan Tedders, his lean countenance drawn into vicious lines, and no sign of his usual lightness, snapped: "I hope, sir, you're going to let the city of the fishmen have some of our beautiful torpedoes."

Kenlon did not reply. The statement, the hatred behind each word jarred, then disturbed him. It was startling to realize that he had not even thought of attacking the city. Frowning, he turned his attention to the approaching craft. It had made a little headway. Watching it, a new thought struck him: in his previous calculations, only the very large vessel had worried him. And yet, the first sign of life and action had come from one of the smaller vessels.

It might be wise to devote study, not only to the thousand-foot giant but to the smaller ships as well. After all, an outsider would regard the *Sea Serpent* as belonging to the smaller craft and dismiss it as unimportant beside the zeppelin. Yet three well-placed torpedoes from the sub's tubes would sink any ship anywhere.

Altogether, there were five of the smaller machines, and each had an un-twentieth-century quality in its design. The one farthest away was hard to see clearly. It seemed to be simply a torpedo-shaped vessel, lying very low in the water. Its visible length was something over a hundred feet. Kenlon had the impression that part of each end was under water and that it was actually a much longer ship.

Three of the remaining four craft didn't look more than a hundred feet long. But they were all different, one from the other. One looked very trim, very streamlined, blue in color. A second had two shining towers that rose up like masts from the deck and towered to a ridiculous height. The third of the smaller ships was a globe about eighty feet in diameter that floated very high in the water and had no visible portholes. It lay there, a dully gleaming ball of metal.

The remaining ship was the high-decked affair from which the flying boat had come.

Beside Kenlon, Lieutenant Benjamin said, "How near are we going to let them come, sir?"

"Eh?" said Kenlon.

He twisted and stared at the air boat, now drifting along less than two hundred yards away. He felt a brief wonder that it should travel so slowly, but that passed in a sharp reawareness of the meaning of Benjamin's words. He thought vaguely: How close shall we let it come?

Quite frankly, he simply hadn't thought of it as dangerous.

"The way I look at it, sir," Tedders said, "is that these people are in the same box as we are, dragged here in exactly the same way. I don't see us starting to fight our descendants, or are they our ancestors?"

"Exactly!" said Kenlon. But he didn't say it out loud. The boat was a hundred feet away; and a tall, uniformed officer had stood up in the bow. There was no time for detailed thought, or hesitation. Kenlon commanded:

"Mr. Tedders, cover them with one of the ack-acks. Mr. Benjamin, sound the general alert, have half a dozen armed men come on deck, and order speed reduced to four and one half knots."

Kenlon scarcely heard their acknowledgments. For, abruptly, he was feeling very silly about his precautions. The air boat was only a score of feet from the conning tower. The people in it were plainly visible. There were seven of them; and they were all women.

The flying boat bumped gently against the bridge and clung there. Its deck was higher than the streamlined railing, so much higher than the woman, standing up in the bow, loomed above Kenlon.

Her position gave him the impression that she was abnormally tall. Then he saw that it wasn't just her vantage point. She *was* tall. She towered five feet nine . . . ten— six feet . . .

Her uniform was of a thick silky material, very feminine in its texture, yet military. She was military, too, in her face and manner; and her voice, when she spoke, had the clipped quality of assured command. She said in English:

"Greetings to the twentieth century."

Kenlon's mind did a twisting somersault. English. Strangely accented. But English! The thrill that had stirred earlier inside him, and had seemed to die, returned, and this time it came alive.

His stomach, so taut for minutes now, actually for days, his mind black with a hundred mortal worries, loosened, lightened. Suddenly, the violent death of Jones-

Gordon came down to its proper perspective, a grievous but not destroying incident in the life of a fighting man who had stayed on his feet to carry on the fight.

Awareness came to the callousness of his attitude, a sad consciousness of the objectivity of the war training that had made him accept the death of his friend and commander after the shortest possible period of grief and shock. But the reality was that events were unreeling at a reckless pace. All that mattered was . . .

He was here; he, William Rainor Kenlon, American, here in the world of A.D. 24,999, commander now of one of the mightiest war machines of his own age, a mid-twentieth-century U.S. atomic submarine, loaded with twenty-four-inch torpedoes, complete with antiaircraft guns and a seaplane, the whole costly and elongated structure capable of cruising under water for an incredibly long time, and so heavily armored that theoretically the sea was supposed to remain outside even if they found it necessary to go down to a depth of eight hundred feet.

The woman was speaking again, in the language of the winged men this time, a puzzled note in her voice:

"What is the matter? Do you not understand American? Are you one of the barbarian non-Americans of that age?"

Kenlon laughed. He couldn't help it. If this was what subsequent ages believed, then it was easy to see who had won all the wars from World War II on. He said in English:

"I beg your pardon, madam. I was so overcome by the fact that you actually spoke . . . American . . . and that—"

He stopped, struck by the truth of his own words. For a month he and the others had lived in an alien universe, made all the more alien by their mental isolation from the people who lived in it. True, he had learned the langauge of the winged men. The ability to establish halting communication only emphasized the gulf between the two species of human.

That was over. Here were comparative compatriots. What age they came from didn't matter. It must be reasonably close for the language to have held its general form, yet also far enough away to have blurred the fact that the non-American world of his time was not necessarily barbarian.

He parted his lips, but before he could speak the young woman said:

"My name is Dorilee. I am Tenant of the Joannas. guarding the Sessa Clen on her way to her marriage bed. May I come aboard?"

Kenlon heard the last sentence only vaguely. His whole mind was concentrated on the meaning of what she had said. It took a moment to grasp that the strange nouns she had used didn't matter. Here were women soldiers escorting another woman, evidently a personage, to her wedding.

It was not until his thoughts had gone that far that the woman's final sentence penetrated. Simultaneously he saw that she seemed not to expect any assistance, and that she had taken his silence as assent. She vaulted lightly down onto the bridge.

She straightened as tall as he, and smiled a generous smile. Her eyes were hazel, her lips firm, her face a little too long for beauty. She said:

"We have been hearing about you for more than a week now, the suggestion being strong that you were the only one with a ship capable of carrying out the requirements of the winged men."

She glanced curiously along the deck, then into the hatch. "So this is a real, live submarine. The only one I ever saw was in a museum in Greater Clen City and—"

In spite of his intense interest in every word she was saying, Kenlon had to interrupt:

"What you said a moment ago—you say you have been hearing about us for a week?"

The woman faced him again. She seemed to comprehend his meaning instantly. "You have a winged man aboard, have you not?"

"Yes."

"He has been communicating by"—she hesitated over the word—"the kedled waves with his superiors for a

month, though it was only last week that I had learned
the language sufficiently to understand the import of what
was being said." She added: "We discovered a similar
kedled instrument on the winged man who came aboard
our ship. It was woven into the clothes he wears."

Nemmo, Kenlon was thinking, you cunning devil. Not,
he realized after a moment, that it mattered.

"May I go down into your ship?" the woman asked.

Kenlon didn't have to think about that. "No," he said.

The woman seemed undisturbed by the instant rejection.

Then we'd like you to visit our ship," she said. "Perhaps, later, we could go down into yours."

Kenlon automatically doubted that last. It would be unwise. But the invitation—if that was what it was—did a
strange thing somewhere inside his head. The thrilling
sense of excitement that came glazed his vision. He stared
at the woman as through a mist.

"Now?"

"Of course—now!" she said. "The Sessa Clen wants to
talk to you."

Kenlon tried to picture that, but his mind balked. It
was not an unpleasant sensation. The haze of excitement
seemed to grow shinier in his head. Through it all there
was a realization that he had no resistance to the idea.

Indeed, he realized he had to go.

The sooner he sized up the entire situation in this fantastic world of the future the better.

He turned to Benjamin and said, "Lieutenant, you are
in command while I'm gone. Let no one aboard for any
reason."

"Good lord, sir, you're going all by yourself?—I beg
your pardon, Captain."

"It's quite all right," said Kenlon. He stepped close to
the man and said in an arguing tone: "Two persons
would be in as great a danger as one, don't you think?"

"I suppose you're right, sir. But why not send someone
else?"

The suggestion that he not be the one to go shocked
Kenlon. Fantasies were pouring through his mind, visions

of himself actually meeting and talking to people of other times.

It seemed that at the moment the only value of his new rank was that he could assign himself to such duties.

Nonetheless, he continued to argue the matter on a rational basis.

"Lieutenant," he said, "in our time, to whom do intelligence agents report?"

Benjamin hesitated; then: "I don't know what you're getting at, sir," he confessed.

"They report to men who have the past experience to evaluate the data that is sent in—correct?"

"I see. We have no such person here."

"None at all, Lieutenant. Hence, the chief has to go himself, as you will discover if something happens to me and the command devolves upon you. I'll keep in touch with you by two-way radio."

"Well—" said Benjamin doubtfully.

Kenlon had enough. "I'm going," he said loudly. "That's settled. Understand about letting no one aboard?"

"Yes, Captain."

Kenlon raised his voice even more, so that the woman could hear: "And if anybody tries to bargain with you over me, the answer is no. We trade nothing for me. Got it?"

Benjamin saluted. "Naturally," he said. His tone of voice said that he meant it.

Kenlon said to the woman, "You'll have to wait a few minutes, while I prepare."

He went below; and among the devices he took with him were a service automatic, a tiny two-way transistor radio, and his compass-watch.

He washed his face and hands, packed his shaving kit, and headed for the deck. Moments later, he was climbing gingerly aboard the aircraft.

He felt a brief tug, but that was the only indication of movement. He looked back. There was open water between the aircraft and the submarine.

Slowly, the gap between the two ships widened.

Chapter 9

It was about twenty minutes later that Kenlon became aware that the Tenant was gazing anxiously off to his left and somewhat behind him. She caught his glance.

"That ship," she said, "is coming in this direction. I think they're trying to head us off."

Kenlon swung around. He saw at once that it was the vessel which had the two metal structures rising from its deck to what seemed an overbalancing height. The craft was sweeping toward them at a speed that rivaled that of a destroyer, to Kenlon's practiced eye.

Its course would, he saw, intercept the path of the aircraft he was on about a quarter of a mile ahead.

Kenlon faced the leader of the Joannas. He pointed up, and said, "Rise above them."

The woman's heavy face remained intent. She shook her head. "This ship was designed with many restrictions," she said, "so that no one would ever be tempted to an illegal abuse in connection with it. It can rise only to about a hundred feet."

Since the "masts"—if that was what they were—of the other machine were only eighty feet, it seemed to Kenlon to be an ample margin.

"Get up there," he commanded.

She began: "Suppose they shoot us down—" She stopped. She shook her head at him in a chastising manner. "Mr. Kenlon, I'm in command of this vessel. I hope you will grant me that."

It was an issue Kenlon was not prepared to contest. He watched silently as the two craft came toward each other. He was aware of the Tenant saying something to one of the Joannas, who pressed a button on the metal beside her. Under Kenlon, the forward drive of the airship ceased. It slowly drifted to a halt. Kenlon and Dorilee walked forward to the railing.

As Kenlon watched, a door opened in the other vessel and two men in bathing suits came out of it. They stood near the opening. One held a little device in his hand; he spoke into it what seemed to be single words. The strange craft came up close to them, then backed water in a way that indicated that it was not a propeller-driven craft, for it stopped short. But it was the other man who walked forward. Kenlon had noticed that there was a cord of some kind around this man's neck, which was attached to a small black, round object. The man now raised the black object and spoke into it. As he did so, a speaker in one of the towers addressed them in a tongue that sounded familiar, but Kenlon did not understand it.

Beside him, Dorilee said, "Oh, he has a translation machine. Good."

She raised her voice and answered.

The interchange continued for some minutes. Kenlon could see that the Tenant was disturbed and the man insistent. Kenlon tugged at the sleeve of the woman's uniform.

"What does he want?"

"You."

Kenlon was astonished. "What for?"

The man on the other vessel fell silent, as Dorilee said uneasily, "His name is Robairst, and—translating into your time terminology—I gather he and his friend are from 6842 A.D. Their attitude is that we—that is I and my group—are taking an advantage of the other people from the past by getting control of you."

She spoke reluctantly. Kenlon gave her a searching look, and there was no doubt in his mind that the two men from the sixty-ninth century A.D. had correctly analyzed *her* intention, at least.

"They're insisting that I let you have a conversation with them," the Tenant said unhappily.

Kenlon was intrigued. "Why not?"

The tall, powerful woman said darkly, "Who knows what they have in mind?"

The meaning of the words, it seemed to Kenlon probably applied as much to her as to the men.

"We all face the same problem—to get home," he said. "No one is going to do anything to jeopardize that."

On the deck below, the men were evidently becoming impatient. One yelled something sharply. She answered resignedly, then turned to Kenlon. "Theirs is a sporting ship and they have weapons superior to ours. I told him they could have you for thirty minutes."

"Why don't you come along?"

The Tenant answered gloomily that she had suggested that. But that the men did not trust her.

It occurred to Kenlon that he had had the same reaction to her. But he said nothing.

He realized that the aircraft was edging forward over the ship. A ladder flowed up from the deck below; it poised in mid-air, waited for the gunwale of the airship to touch it. At the moment of touch, the other ship matched speed. The ladder rubbed noisily against the metal. But it felt solid to Kenlon as he swung himself over, and began to edge down it.

He reached the deck below without mishap and looked around him eagerly.

A sporting ship!

He would have liked to pause and examine the towers, ask questions, discover mechanical details. But the larger of the two men—Robairst—pointed at the open doorway.

He spoke into his microphone, and the remarkable translating speaker—which a minute before had spoken the Clen language—now said in English, "In here, Mr. Kenlon."

The interior was—sunlit. The walls that had seemed so opaque on the outside were as transparent as air from the inside. There *were* barriers to his vision, but they were protrusions and extrusions inside the vessel itself.

The furnishings were those of a comfortable lounge. That vaguely surprised Kenlon. Exactly what he had expected, he couldn't have said.

Yet, as he saw the chairs and settees, he actually had the thought: Of course, what else! In A.D. 6842 human beings still had legs and arms, still had to sit, lie down, sleep and eat, and evidently they still enjoyed fishing. In fact, if there was any difference at all between the twentieth-century and the sixty-ninth-century man, it was not immediately apparent.

"Have a seat!" said a translating speaker hidden in the wall to his left.

Kenlon sank down into a settee. After a moment, the older and more heavily built of his hosts—Robairst—sat down, also. The younger man remained standing.

He was sharp-faced, sharp nosed, and angular of body. He was clearly finding it hard to restrain himself, for he said finally to his companion, "Shall I begin?"

Robairst said, "This is my associate, Tainar."

Tainar seemed to take that as the cue, for he said, "Mr. Kenlon, the other people from the past who have been brought to this era without their consent, have been here longer than you. Half of us are under severe pressure to return to our own time, and with one or two exceptions, we are in full agreement as to the course you should pursue with your submarine."

He spread his hands in a gesture of frustration. "It would be very disturbing to the majority of us if you now, in your own good time, examined the situation, considered the pros and cons, and finally did anyway what we consider inevitable. We want you to say that you will carry out the majority decision and destroy the fishermen's city."

The bigger man surged to his feet. "Just a minute," he said. "I don't think you've presented our position with enough force."

He turned to Kenlon, said quickly, "We're businessmen, Mr. Kenlon. We were at the end of our vacation when this"—he waved in the direction of the winged men's eyrie—"this ridiculous thing happened to us. For three weeks now we have been overdue in our offices. So we stand to lose our status. You can see how serious our predicament is."

It didn't seem particularly serious to Kenlon. He must be missing something in their situation.

He also had an uneasy feeling that he himself was in more danger than the outward appearance of the scene indicated.

So he parried: "Why don't you tell me a little more about your own era and this urgency you feel?"

The two men exchanged glances. Then Tainar said flatly, "If my partner and I don't return at once to our time, the government will turn our business over to other qualified persons. We stand to lose the kind of income that enables us to support seagoing craft of this caliber. If that happens, our names go to the bottom of the qualifying list."

The picture Kenlon got was that in the sixty-ninth century a business could not be owned. It was assigned to a "qualified" manager, who operated it for his own profit. Evidently, under certain circumstances, the executive could lose his "job" to another qualified person.

"Is that it?" he asked.

It was, the men agreed.

Tainar finished grimly, "I should call to your attention that the human thought that Robairst and I represent is based on more data and upon five thousand years more of experience than was available in your own age. For that reason, you should follow our advice without argument."

Kenlon was offended by the implied imputation of inferiority. Restraining his irritation, he said quietly, "By that reasoning, we ought to consult the respresentatives, singular or plural, of the oldest civilization here, and find out what he or they think."

A pained look came into Tainar's thin face. "That nut!" he said contemptuously.

"Well, then, the second oldest," said Kenlon.

On the settee opposite Kenlon, Robairst cleared his throat and stood up. "All right," he said, and all the surface goodwill was gone from his voice and manner, "I guess we have to speak plainly. Yes or no?"

Kenlon drew a deep breath. He had a strong feeling that the moment of crisis had come. But he couldn't even

imagine agreeing that the welfare of two men was sufficient argument for him to destroy a city, in which tens of
thousands of fish-humans dwelt.

"No!" he said curtly.

During the long pause that ensued, Kenlon found his
gaze wandering beyond his hosts to the open water outside. He could feel that the ship he was in was cruising
slowly. Its motion had brought into partial view the large,
ball-like machine, which was now much closer than it had
been when he last saw it; it was not more than a hundred
and fifty yards distant. However, no sign of actvity
showed.

Kenlon grew aware that the two men in the lounge had
drawn together and were standing side by side gazing at
him somberly.

"Commander Kenlon," Robairst said, "we hope you realize that there is no legal restraint in this era to which
any of us need pay attention."

Kenlon said in a formal tone, "The officers and men of
the U.S.S. *Sea Serpent* will conduct themselves according
to rules and regulations governing conduct of our own
time."

Tainar turned to his friend, spread his palms and
hands. "You see," he said, "it'll be six months before he
starts thinking."

He broke off, and, turning to Kenlon, said in an icy
voice, "I have to tell you it's a case of agree—or die!"

Kenlon had been bracing himself for some kind of ultimatum. Now, he sighed. "Suppose I agree, and then don't
do it—when I get back to my ship?" He shrugged. "Let's
face all the realities."

Tainar smiled tautly. "You *are* going back to your ship,
Mr. Kenlon. When you go, there will be attached to your
skin in one armpit a tiny metal capsule, the kind we use
to shoot big fish under water. Once this capsule is attached to a fish, it is difficult to dislodge. And if it is
dislodged, it promptly explodes whereupon the dead fish
floats to the surface—"

Robairst interrupted fiercely, "If within forty-eight
hours of returning to your ship, you have not made the

attack on the fishmen's city, we will explode the capsule by remote control. That, Mr. Kenlon, is what I tried to avoid by my initial appeal to your good sense."

Kenlon stood up, said coolly, "All right, you'd better put your fish tag on me and let me be on my way." He added, "I won't bother to tell you my opinion of you two s.o.b.'s."

Tainar seemed not to hear. Deliberately, he walked over to one wall, pulled open a drawer, and in a gingerly fashion took out a pair of tongs. There was a glint of something between the two hands of the instrument, as he carried it toward Kenlon.

Without glancing around, he held one hand out to his partner. "Give me the padding."

Silently, Robairst stepped forward and placed a flat, flexible, brown object in the outstretched fingers. Then he stepped back and continued his alert watch.

Tainar held the brown padding out to Kenlon, who accepted it. The man said, "Remove your coat and other clothing, and place it under your right armpit. Then I'll attach the capsule."

As Kenlon hesitated, Robairst's voice urged, "I strongly recommend you use the padding, Captain. Clothing is not a sufficient protection. Remember, this capsule was made to cling to the tough hide of a shark or other big fish."

Kenlon believed him.

Reluctantly, he started to unbutton his coat. And he actually had his arm out of one sleeve—when it happened.

In front of him, Tainar collapsed on the floor.

Kenlon saw from the corner of one eye that Robairst had dropped in the same instant fashion.

Both men lay like dead objects on the thick matting.

There was a rattling sound from the hidden speaker. Then a man's voice said, "Commander Kenlon, we're watching this scene from the round ship. We ask you to act quickly, because those two will shortly return to consciousness. Go on deck. We will switch voice translation control over to a deck speaker."

Out on the deck, Kenlon needed only a moment to orient himself.

The aircraft of the henchmen of the Sessa Clen was off to his left about four hundred yards. Except for the round ship, the other vessels were still far away. Their distance gave him the feeling, whether false or true, that they were not forces that needed to be reckoned with at this time.

As Kenlon waited tensely, an opening appeared in the lustrous metal of the huge globe. A kind of balcony slid out. Three men in simple one-piece uniforms and a girl in what seemed to be a bathing suit came out onto this structure.

Abruptly, the "balcony" detached itself from the ship and glided through the air toward Kenlon. It traversed the intervening space in less than a minute and came to a halt in a hovering position over the deck of the fishing vessel. Two of the men and the girl stepped down near Kenlon. The third man remained on the tiny craft.

One of the men who had come down to the deck was of medium height, and lean-faced. With a faint, sympathetic smile, he handed Kenlon a tiny object.

Kenlon saw that the man had a similar object, into which he now spoke.

"Address us through that microphone," the man said. "The message has to go back to our ship before it is transmitted to their translation computer and speaker system."

Kenlon heard and nodded his understanding. But his attention was not on the words. Utterly fascinated, he walked up to the little airship, where it poised effortlessly in the air. He put his hand out, glanced questioningly at the young man aboard and—when there was no negative reaction—fingered the side of the craft.

It felt slightly warm to the touch. But there was not a tremor of vibration—suggesting that some kind of solid state mechanism was involved, one without moving parts.

Kenlon looked up at the young man, raised his own microphone, and spoke into it. "How does it work?"

Behind him, the speaker in the mast translated his

question into what was presumably the language of these four people.

The man on the aircraft smiled faintly, but after only a moment's hesitation he answered: "I'm going to guess that you can comprehend a technical summary."

As he described it then, the interaction of forces in atoms and similar particles had been examined over the millennia with ever greater exactness. He said, "You may remember from your own knowledge of physics that certain nuclear particles had a half-life of only a fraction of a second."

Kenlon recalled peering into cloud chambers and at photographic plates on which tiny streaks of light revealed—it had been said—that a particle traveling at tens of thousands of miles per second had been formed by a nuclear reaction, had made a journey of eight inches, more or less, and had then dissipated, its force spent.

"Methods," said his mentor—"meaning mostly proper environments—were created whereby such particles could increase their half-life to respectable ages like one second, or even longer."

Thus it had been possible to explore their properties and capabilities.

"For example"—the explanation continued—"this ship is operated by a multiple system whereby one such particle, called the Beta Z, is so channeled that it and its companions have a half-life of about one and three-quarter seconds."

Given this substantial existence in time, they altered the normal condition of space in their immediate vicinity. While that condition was maintained, any object affected by it—such as a ship—acted as if it were operating in free space.

"I see," said Kenlon. And it seemed to him that he did see, dimly and with much respect, how many thousands, and perhaps millions, of hours of research would be required to duplicate the engine of this vessel.

Before he could speak again, one of the men on the deck touched his shoulder. Kenlon turned; and the man said into another of the tiny mikes, "Mr. Kenlon, Robairst and Tainar will awaken in about five minutes. So let us not waste any time here. First, let me introduce my friends and myself."

The girl's name was Lidadeeda, the man beside her Camforay, and the man on their little aircraft, Massagand. The tall man gave his name as Tulgoronet and said that they were from the Setidillad era of human history.

"As best we can calculate," said Tulgoronet earnestly, "we come from roughly eighty-six hundred years after the twentieth century—about 10,650 A.D."

Their round ship was actually a spaceship, an interplanetary research laboratory, which had landed in the water near an earth city. While there, a winged man had attached his time travel plates and had come aboard.

"Before we could nullify what he was up to," said Tulgoronet ruefully, "we were here."

A spaceship!

The information, the implication, was so sensational that Kenlon thought: They'll have all that information. Detailed knowledge of the planets and an account of the history of civilization going back, back, back . . .

At that point his thought was interrupted, as the girl uttered words into her microphone. The fact that the translating machine spoke in a woman's voice was immediately interesting to Kenlon and drew his attention to her.

The girl said in an urgent tone, "We had better take Commander Kenlon"—she glanced directly at Kenlon—"either to your submarine or to the Sessa Clen's air carriage."

Kenlon offered no resistance to their haste. But as he climbed aboard he indicated the other vessels. "Have you looked into all those ships with the spy ray, which is what I'm guessing you used to see into Robairst's and Tainar's ship?"

It was Massagand who replied: "All except one. That ship over there"—he pointed—"was not reachable by our technique."

Kenlon gazed in the direction indicated, and, after accustoming his eyes to the light and shade of the flickering water, saw that the man had pointed at the large torpedo shape which, of all these vessels, most clearly resembled his own submarine.

Beside Kenlon, Lidadeeda said urgently, "Where to, Commander? We want to leave before these two come to consciousness."

Kenlon, sensing the impatience of his rescuers, said, "Take me to the Sessa Clen's—what did you call it?—air carriage."

A minute and a half later, he was deposited at his destination. Kenlon stood and waved, as the craft darted off in a curving path, uneeringly back to the opening in the round vessel.

It attached itself, slid inside, and then the opening slowly glided shut.

Chapter 10

Kenlon turned and saw that the Joanna, Dorilee, had come beside him.

"I was beginning to get worried about you," she said. "What did they want?"

"They want me to destroy the city of the fishmen," he said.

"Did you agree?" Her big, handsome face showed an alert interest.

It struck Kenlon that the Clen probably also wanted the fish city wrecked. He said evasively, "I told them I would take it under advisement."

"And the others—from the round ship?"

"They wanted to meet me," Kenlon said.

His explanation seemed to satisfy her, for she turned away and gave an order. The airship began to move again. In their slow fashion they came presently to the main ship of the Sessa Clen, red-hued, standing high above the waves.

Close up, it was revealed to be a surprisingly large vessel, as big as a good-sized yacht. Kenlon estimated its length at nearly two hundred feet. The air carriage settled down into a cavity in the deck.

Dorilee hurried off, talked briefly to another big woman in an officer's uniform, then called out to him to come. As Kenlon stepped onto the main deck, Dorilee joined him, breathless. "We must hurry," she said. "We mustn't keep the Sessa Clen waiting."

Kenlon did not resist but walked behind her along two corridors and down one flight of steps. They came to a door that opened into what in other ships would have been called a passenger lounge.

The room was large and brilliantly lighted. About fifty ladies, all dressed in red and white striped gowns were standing along the two opposite walls. Powerful Joannas—he estimated thirty of them—stood at various doorways and formed in two ranks at the far end of the room.

Kenlon's gaze took in these details quickly; and then he fixed his attention where the others were fixing theirs.

A young, slender, blond woman in an all-scarlet dress sat in a chair at that distant end of the room. The chair was on a dais, which raised her more than a foot above the floor.

At first look, she seemed little more than a girl. But as Kenlon followed Dorilee across the room and saw the Sessa Clen's face more clearly, he estimated her age at twenty-five or perhaps even a year or two more.

His thought reached that point; and then Dorilee, who had stopped, and stepped aside, motioned him forward. Kenlon continued on until he was about eight feet from the blond woman, and then he stopped also.

Several moments passed before he realized that he had carried through with the entire ritual, which by implication acknowledged the superiority that was being presented him.

Kenlon hesitated. But it was a little hard to know how to avoid the reality of this royal court without giving offense.

The Sessa Clen inclined her head at him.

Kenlon presumed that he had been officially recognized. He bowed, then straightened.

At close range, the woman's thin face was very distinctive looking. It struck him that part of that distinctiveness was stamped there by an inner sense of power, which radiated from her.

Before he could think further, she spoke in her own language. Her voice was deep and husky rather than musical.

From behind Kenlon, Dorilee translated, "Commander, the Sessa Clen welcomes you to her royal ship and re-

quests that, since she was on her way to her marriage bed
when this ship was seized by the winged men, that you
take your submarine and destroy the undersea city, so
that she and her entourage can resume their proper journey."

Kenlon sighed. So it was to be as direct as that. So be
it. "I refuse!" he said.

There was silence; then Dorilee said to him in a
shocked voice, "I can't translate that, Commander."

The Sessa must have realized that something was
amiss, for she spoke sharply to the Tenant. With reluctance in every tone, Dorilee thereupon spoke. Suddenly, a
collective gasp came from all parts of the room—and
Kenlon judged that his refusal had been correctly communicated.

In front of him, the blond woman stood up, visibly agi-
tated. She spoke several sentences in a high-pitched voice,
then turned, headed for the door, and walked through it
into the corridor beyond. She was briefly visible, then she
was gone from sight.

Dorilee said to Kenlon in a trembling voice, "The Sessa
Clen realizes that your statement was dictated by igno-
rance of protocol in connection with such a person as herself. She wishes me to inform you that for this reason
your words will not be held against you."

Kenlon recognized that the message was conciliatory,
but it was also clear that the Sessa was accustomed to her
slightest whim being obeyed.

He was anxious to depart. The atmosphere depressed
him. And, besides, there were other ships to visit.

Silently, he followed Dorilee back the way they had
come.

As he emerged on deck, Kenlon looked for the sun.
But in his absence, the sky had again clouded over. The
sun was locatable only by a vague brightness in the over-
cast, and that could have been an illusion.

Kenlon walked to the railing and indicated the three
ships lying in the distance, starboard. To his far left was
the biggest of all the vessels that had been brought to this
time. Almost straight ahead was a trim-looking blue

yacht, and, finally, the long, dark craft that looked like a submarine without a conning tower.

"Who's in them?" he asked.

Dorilee's big handsome face twisted into a frown. "No one's been able to contact the one that lies so low in the water," she said. "There's one man in the blue ship. He's a peaceful type from a period much later than the Clen time. He's very powerful in some way, but not threatening. As for the big ship—"

Her frown deepened. Then she explained reluctantly that the big vessel was the *Segomay 8* from the year A.D. 2852, and that its all-male crew had already made unpleasant threats and advances in connection with the large number of women in the Sessa Clen's entourage.

"We won't take you over there," she finished. "But they have one of those automatic translating systems; so you could talk to Captain Gand, if you wish."

She must have seen from his face that he wanted very much to have such a conversation. For she yelled an order in her own language. A short time later, one of her Joannas handed Kenlon a small microphone; and Dorilee said, "Captain Gand is on the other end."

Kenlon held the tiny microphone close to his mouth and said, "Hello, Captain—this is Kenlon, commander of the submarine."

The words that came back to him from the microphone were spoken in a baritone in an extremely colloquial tone of cynical admiration:

"So you've already got aboard the Sessa Clen's ship. Say, that's fast work. Hey, Kenlon, are those dames pretty?"

Kenlon said he hadn't noticed.

"Not that it matters," Captain Gand continued. "If we could figure out some way"—he stopped, broke off gloomily: "It's a sad situation, Commander, when people like you and me have to realize that we come from primitive times and that a gang of women have a superior science. Even that little air carriage has got plenty of stuff on it."

"Stuff?" echoed Kenlon. It seemed an obvious word but he felt the need for clarification.

"We tried to hook it with a tractor beam," said Captain Gand indignantly. "First thing you know they had our tractors sucking up sea water. My engineers can't figure how they did that."

Kenlon, who was interested in advanced science, nevertheless had as his main purpose finding out what was the equipment of Gand's own vessel. It required a few minutes of questioning, but presently he had his picture.

The *Segomay 8* was equipped to set down and dismantle undersea installations. It was a maintenance ship for the machines and way stations that dotted the ocean bottom of the twenty-ninth century, and it supplied a number of the nearly one thousand undersea mining operations that maintained year-round work shifts. But it had nothing that could act against the undersea city of the fishmen.

"We tried," said Gand in a bitter tone, "but it was easy for them to cut off the tools we lowered."

Aloud, Kenlon surmised from the statement that Gand favored extermination of the fishmen.

"Of course!" The baritone voice sounded surprised. Gand added grimly, "My owners are losing money every day that I'm here, and I'm going to have a hard time explaining where I've been. So don't wait too long before you make up your mind. How about it?"

Kenlon said that before he decided he wanted also to talk to the people aboard the blue craft and the dark ship. He finished in a puzzled tone. "I've got to admit I have neglected to ask this question, but when we finally go back why can't we just be set down a minute or two after we left? That way nobody will have to explain anything."

"Oh, no," said Gand, "that's impossible."

"Why?"

As Gand explained it, then, briefly, no matter-state was ever the same from one instant to the next. Thus the matter-energy complex of every atom in their vessels continued its normal evolvement through time. Because of that force rigidity, it would be impossible for an object to break through the barriers thus created. Which was fortunate, because it would instantly disappear if impingement actually occurred.

Gand ended his account in a baffled tone: "You'll have to get Arpo to explain the details to you."

"Arpo?"

"He's in that blue vessel. He's a harmless guy—but smart—from way up there in the future. He's neutral in this whole thing. In fact"—his tone was suddenly scathing—"he's so altruistic, he doesn't even mind being here. Imagine that."

He concluded in a matter-of-fact tone: "Nobody's been able to raise a reaction from that other ship, the one that lies so low in the water."

Beside Kenlon, Dorilee said, "We've been trying to contact Arpo. But there's no reply."

At that moment, a thought formed in Kenlon's mind. It said, "Commander, purely as a courtesy, I give you my best wishes. But there's nothing I can do for you."

As that thought came through, there came with it an overtone of love feeling. It was a pure force, so powerful that Kenlon felt his whole body change in a peculiar, joyful sympathy.

Then he thought: Oh, my God, I've got to get some information from him.

All this happened so naturally; it was such a complete communication, and so quick, that only after Kenlon had responded with total acceptance did the reality of what was here strike through to him.

Mental telepathy . . . Perfect.

. . . This was the man that Tainar had called a "nut."

Alongside of the love feeling, Kenlon sensed some enormous potential of brain power.

The frantic feeling came back with a rush at that point. "What, what, what—" thought Kenlon wildly.

Arpo must have been waiting for him to complete his series of reactions, for again, as clearly as before, his thought came into Kenlon's mind.

"Perhaps," Arpo said, "the best thing I can do for you is to give you a brief history of mankind."

Kenlon snatched at that as if he were in stormy waters clutching for a lifeline. "Yes, yes."

And so he had his first history of civilization.

Scientifically, most of the realities underlying the physical nature of the tangible universe were fairly well documented by the thirty-eighth century A.D. At that time certain complexities in the behavior of particles yielded a new view of nature that made it possible to modify the basic theory.

Such modification had to do with the discovery that particles statistically followed rules of behavior but as an individual a particle was capable of making a choice. The choice involved was not of the same level as a life form "deciding" to go north instead of south, or of Peter choosing to marry Joanna instead of Anne. But its rule was a peculiar version of could—maybe—this?—that?—why not?—O.K.

The particle had about a 90 percent effective built-in assumption that all directions were equally worthwhile. So why not go *there?*—usually the sanest way. It was found possible to alter this assumption by techniques.

At that point, control of nature took on a different, fantastic, but compelling and accelerated meaning.

In the realm of human relations, on the one hand a small group of scientists virtually solved the entire psychological equation in terms of understanding it. But individual man in mass could not be made—except rarely—to confront himself. The six billion inhabitants of thirtieth-century earth, the three billion of the fiftieth century, the sixteen billion of the sixty-fifth century—the peak population of the planet—and the two billion of the eighty-fifty century—almost uniformly revealed that the impulse might be understood in terms of internal energy flows and neural center pre-programing—but man was too numerous; the great mass of him could not be caged by any system. Could not be trained, could not be conditioned, educated, altered, except painstakingly one person at a time. And that was impossible.

So the deadly wars continued periodically and pitilessly.

The conquerors endlessly battered earth's cities and gave no peace that all men could accept.

The change came when the ancestors of Arpo, probably the result of mutation, began to show up in an area that had suffered heavily from radiation. They followed an absolute principle of goodwill and nonresistance. War ended.

Peace came.

Arpo could only surmise that when the great lands began to sink into the ocean in the deluge that had produced the winged men and the fishmen, that the descendants of his own era had made no more resistance to it than they had to invaders in earlier millennia.

"And now, Commander," Arpo concluded, "I will answer one question, no more."

Kenlon, whose mind was seething with questions, gulped in his excitement. For a moment, then, he felt like a man to whom a genie has given a single wish. His brain seemed to soar to an infinite height. Then it came down to earth again as he realized his duty and his basic purpose.

He glanced hurriedly over toward the low-lying vessel, barely visible under that dull sky. He urgently projected the thought, his question: "Who's in there—in that dark ship?" He added, "I'd like to go there and talk to them."

"I can't read them," Arpo's thought came. "They've put up a barrier so advanced, it would disarrange my present internal balance to force through. And I choose not to do that."

"You could?"

"Yes," said Arpo. "And with that, I'll say goodbye and good luck."

"Wait!" said Kenlon. "Do you have any advice about the fishmen and the winged—"

Even as he was asking the question, he *felt* the mind withdraw.

The effect on him was like the sudden separation from a very dear person. It left him sad, as if he had suffered a loss. Kenlon turned to Dorilee and said in a subdued tone: "I guess you'd better take me back to my ship."

Chapter 11

At dusk it started to rain. Kenlon put on his rain garb and went up on the narrow deck of the submarine, turned his face upward and let the wetness come down on him. The raindrops felt cool and delightful. But more important by far was that, to his experienced eye, this had the look of being an all-night rain.

Darkness descended on the near watery horizon with an almost totally black effect. The waves had their own little brightnesses, but actual visibility was a matter of a few feet or yards.

He returned to his quarters, slept for five hours; and then arose, shaved, and gave the order that started the machine on its dive and into forward motion.

In the darkness, utilizing his careful daytime calculations, he guided the *Sea Serpent* in a wide, circling course that took the submarine all the way around the other ships. When he reached a point that he conceived to be due north of the submarine-like craft, he came up to the periscope depth and headed south at the slowest speed of which the undersea ship was capable. The propellers barely turned over.

Then he went to the conning tower.

Benjamin, who was there, merely shook his head, wonderingly, when he saw that Kenlon was dressed for the water. Kenlon understood the resigned expression in his senior officer's face, and he said, "After all, I started as a scuba diver."

"All I can say, sir," said Benjamin, "is that you have my respect."

Kenlon argued, "We absolutely have to check these

people. Not to do so would leave an Intelligence vacuum."

"Indeed it would, sir," said Lieutenant Benjamin in a tactful tone of voice.

Without another word being spoken, Benjamin gave the commands that brought the sub to a lying-to position, with conning tower awash.

Kenlon and the two Scuba men who were to accompany him went out the top and over into the dark sea outside.

The water was tropical warm. Kenlon swam with the others, quietly. In the relative security of the calm sea they moved with scarcely a ripple; the rain pelted them in a sudden, sustained downpour. The night, already black as pitch, seemed to grow even blacker.

... Black water below, black night ahead and above.

Kenlon had always felt peaceful in water, and gradually now his tension faded.

But he kept count of the minutes by an intuitive mechanism in his head. When it seemed to him that the exact correct time had gone by, he reached toward his companions, and touched the leg of one, the arm of the other.

Forward swimming ceased. They trod water. Kenlon took it for granted that the two men were getting their night glasses out of the cases strapped to their backs. He did the same. A few minutes later, he was staring at the strange scene.

His timing had been accurate.

The torpedo-shaped vessel was scarcely thirty feet away.

But something far more sensational was happening.

On that hitherto deserted deck, with the rain coming down, there was movement.

As Kenlon trod water and stood, so to say, on his fins, paddling gently, he saw several figures crawl up from the water into the strange craft.

He thought, amazed: They've been having a swim in the dark.

Considering the rain, the secrecy of it was a revelation, presumably of fear.

He felt a certain tolerance. In a way it was natural. The truth probably was that everybody who had been brought here from the past ought to be absolutely petrified with fear.

. . . More movement on the deck. A structure rose up from the flat surface. In appearance it resembled a conning tower.

Seeing it, realizing that an entrance was being made for the swimmers, Kenlon suppressed a strong impulse to go aboard and introduce himself before it was too late.

Not now, he decided. Not in this darkness.

After a moment, he was appalled at the easy, almost unresisted way in which the thought-feeling had passed through his mind, and how, instantly, he had wanted to act on it.

The thought ended; for the figures that had crawled up onto the deck of the strange vessel were climbing to their feet, first one, then four more.

Kenlon stared, fascinated, through his night glasses. The rain seemed to distort the figures. Shape, structure, even way of movement, was affected by his perception of them through the watery streaks on the lens through which he gazed.

He was about to comment, to give the next signal—when it struck him that even rain had never before caused such a perceptual effect.

Then he realized.

They were not men.

The best impression Kenlon had was that a number of small crocodiles had stood up on long legs and had walked and moved with a flexibility and assurance that no earthly crocodiles would ever be capable of.

The enormous shock of his discovery ran its course through his nervous system. There remained in him a sense of heightened, unpleasant stimulation.

But it all narrowed down to a practical question: What now?

He found himself realizing ruefully that what he had seen could make no difference.

The nature of military action was that it required logic

that transcended human impulse. Where instinct said, "Get the hell out of here!" military logic commanded aggressive reconnaissance.

Since his companions had also been gazing through *their* special night binoculars, Kenlon merely fumbled for and grabbed each man's hand in turn, and whispered, "Did you see them?"

A squeeze of the hand indicated yes.

"O.K., let's measure the ship, as planned."

That was military logic.

And they went forward. And they dived under the vessel.

It was fifty feet in diameter at its widest, about forty feet thick, and a hundred and twenty feet long.

It had no visible drive mechanism—no rocket tubes, no propellers, nothing at all to mar the surface, no openings of any kind.

Kenlon remembered what Arpo had said—about the advanced energy fields that guarded this ship even from Arpo. He surmised that motion was achieved within the frame of a "field." It was only a deduction, but there had to be something that propelled.

It was very frustrating to have not a single clue as to what that something might be.

Reluctantly, finally, Kenlon gave the signal to retreat.

As soon as he was aboard the *Sea Serpent*, Kenlon called Benjamin and Tedders to the captain's quarters and described what the other scuba divers and he had seen.

"Well, gentlemen, what do you think?" he finished. "What do you make of it? More important, what shall we do?"

There was silence, then Benjamin said, "Captain, did you ask any of the people aboard these other vessels if contact had been established with alien civilizations in other star systems in their time?"

Kenlon had to confess that the thought had not even crossed his mind. He also admitted that he did not see what Benjamin was driving at.

"Why, sir, that a visiting alien spaceship was inadvertently brought here to the future by a winged man."

"Oh!" said Kenlon.

He sat there, contemplating that perfectly simple explanation. Of course. What else?

"For Pete's sake," he said, "I've been an idiot. Bring Nemmo up here."

Nemmo came.

"We have not been able to contact our winged companion who brought that vessel here," Nemmo said. "We have the unhappy feeling that, after fastening the time cups, he was unable to get aboard and so was left behind."

Despite the other's sad tone, Kenlon's reaction was the beginning of relief. Nevertheless, he persisted. "But this ship was definitely brought from the past?"

"Oh, yes. After its arrival the cups were plainly visible on it for several hours. Apparently, these people were then able to remove them—which is very skillful of them. It shows an advanced technical knowledge. Arpo could have done it, but of course he would not resist or interfere."

Kenlon considered the explanation—which now seemed complete—and said finally, delighted, "Well, that solves the whole problem. Now we know our next move."

"What?" asked Benjamin warily.

Kenlon grinned. "We go to bed."

But he was up again shortly after dawn.

Chapter 12

The submarine, running awash under a still murky sky, finally reversed propellers and came to a halt about a mile from the torpedo-shaped vessel of the aliens.

Kenlon had the powered skiff lowered into the water with himself in it. As soon as he was cast free, he started the motor and set forth on his lonely voyage.

It was a strange journey, for he had many thoughts. The great scene around him was, of course, now familiar: There were the other craft, far enough away so that it could have been a setting in any era of man, the timeless sea, rippling, roaring, with whitening waves, and the endless, watery horizon—these also belonged to all the ages of man.

But out of the corner of his eye he kept seeing the eyrie of the winged men—an incredible structure; its presence jarred on the otherwise normal-appearing environment of the vast ocean, which for so many years had been his second home.

It kept stirring in him a foolish thought. Me—here? It was his child reaction to things, a sort of—can this really be happening to me?

Yet now, as in the past, he noticed that he was deliberately seeking the unusual experience. It was not at all a case of being caught by surprise—not any more.

As he studied the low-lying submarine-type vessel, to which he was drawing closer by the minute, he realized that he accepted what Benjamin had said the previous night: these were visitors from space to the earth of long ago.

And the fact that they had been lying-to in some

watery space harbor evidenced that their presence was known to, acknowledged, and accepted by the human beings of that period of history.

Therefore, the time had come to make a determined effort to contact them—openly, without threat. And find out how they might fit into a project for getting everyone back to their proper time.

His little boat had by now come within a couple of hundred yards of the low-lying vessel. Kenlon reversed propellers and coasted even closer on momentum.

As he started forward motion again very slowly, what he had hoped for, happened.

The same structure that had glided into view the night before was rising from the upper surface of the vessel. It came up a good eight feet, higher than Kenlon had remembered it.

It stopped, and a sliding door opened. Out of this stepped, one after the other, three of the creatures.

They stood; his impression of the night before was verified. They looked as if somehow crocodiles had grown to have prehensile legs and arms, and the ability to balance and hold themselves with a casual ease, even grace, and they gazed at Kenlon with eyes that appraised him shrewdly. He could see the quality of intelligence in them even at a hundred feet.

Abruptly, one of the three raised an arm and motioned him to come.

The arm movement, the way the fingers flexed, the significance in the exact mechanism of the action—was human in its meaning. Kenlon had the distinct impression that that was what it was, and that therefore these beings had learned to imitate human motions.

At some depth of his brain, he took it for granted that crocodiles would not normally beckon each other with a take-it-for-granted, calling-toward, arm action.

And since that was how this one did it, Kenlon reassured himself again, these alien beings *were* familiar with man, *had* a long association, *had* learned the ways of human nature—but were probably completely bewildered as to how they had got where they now were—into this age of endless water.

These awarenesses moved rapidly through Kenlon's brain, while he maneuvered his craft forward and alongside the stranger.

One of the lizard men pointed somewhat forward. He moved there, and saw that steps at that point led up from the water, and that there was a series of holes in them, where he could tie his boat.

He tied it, then put his foot down onto the highest step he could reach—which was still several inches under water.

He climbed up, however, onto a runway. He was motioned toward the open door; he walked toward it, and cringed as he edged past the three beings—the closeness of them, the almost face to face look of them, stirred a deep anxiety. His flesh crawled.

And then he was past and entering through the doorway.

He was conscious of the aliens pressing close behind him, and so he moved onto the bare metal floor that was inside, to give them plenty of room.

As he turned, Kenlon saw that the curved door was sliding shut in a solid, smooth fashion that suggested watertight and airtight engineered perfection.

Below him, the floor moved downward. He glanced at his companions, and again he cringed involuntarily.

They made no move, no sound; simply returned his glance, their eyes bright, and brown, and intelligent.

The downward motion ceased. The door glided open in the same silent manner. Through the opening thus made, Kenlon saw a gleaming corridor.

The three lizard men walked through the doorway, then turned and waited for him. Kenlon walked out, past them, past several closed doors, then to another open door.

When he stepped through that, he found himself in a large room.

Nearly a dozen lizard men turned as he entered and looked at him.

Kenlon stopped. He was aware of his three guides crowding close behind him. But their presence made no difference.

He could not bring himself to go forward into the room.

He stood there, almost rooted to the floor. After what seemed a long time, but was probably not more than a few dozen seconds, one of the creature beings detached himself from the group, walked slowly forward, and spoke in a series of grunts and whistles—at least that was what it sounded like to Kenlon.

As the being finished talking, a voice said in English from somewhere in the ceiling—obviously a translation of what had been said by the spokesman:

"Mr. Human Being, we are members of the Yaz race, and we come from a star system in the Milky Way. We comprehend what has happened here—this journey through time, however, caught us by surprise. But we have now analyzed this situation, and we wish to make a deal."

As the translation proceeded, Kenlon felt his tension begin to fade. But he was also puzzled. So when the opening speech was finished, and there was silence again, he said, "How did you know that my language was English?"

The words were translated into grunts and whistles by the ceiling speaker.

The creature, who had addressed Kenlon, said, "We have been following you in your travels, tuning in on your conversation and last night we detected your presence in the water, and caught glimpses of you, and overheard your few words spoken to your companions."

As the meaning of those words came through in the translation, Kenlon had a distinctly unpleasant feeling. It was disconcerting to realize that his moves had been observed by alien eyes, and that last night he and the others had been seen—and, presumably, permitted to complete their exploration.

"You evidently understand water communication," he said.

"We're water people," was the translated reply, "but

this ship is equipped for space travel and very scantily equipped for underwater activity——"

Kenlon was relieved to hear that.

"So we might as well be frank," continued the spokesman. "We're as much in need of you and your ship as the others."

Kenlon was silent. He had the very strong feeling that the *Sea Serpent* and its crew were lucky not to have been taken over by these beings.

The thought came also that this time he had really walked into a trap. He would not easily escape from these beings. He sensed in them purpose without deviation.

But still he did not realize the truth.

As the conversation progressed, he had unfrozen slightly from his tense holding stance. So he was able to shift position, to move his body, to——observe.

He saw that all the creatures were watching him closely. But there was nothing to think about that except what he already had: this time it was for real.

The being in front of him was speaking again, and presently the words came from the translating machine:

"We intend to be even more frank than we already have. We are confronted either by a coincidence of peculiar improbability, or else someone among the winged men knows more than we have suspected. Let me tell you our background——"

Their ship was one of many that had left its home area about 4000 years before. Searching for habitable planets, it was nearly a hundred earth years from its sun when it came to the solar system. The human beings of the time were accustomed to alien visitors, and accepted these newcomers cordially and without suspicion.

Thus the Yaz were able, without interference, to start a transformation in remote areas of the planet, whereby a chain reaction in the atoms of soil and rock broke down the cohesion of the particles. The result was that after a rain, mud remained. A single downpour in an affected area presently converted it into the equivalent of bottomless quicksand, much as he had already seen it . . .

Kenlon heard a high-pitched voice say, "Hey, what are you saying? *You* did this?—all this water?"

Then he realized it was his own voice, and he clamped his mouth shut, and he stood there with a blank, stunned feeling.

The Yaz spokesman continued as if he had not heard: "The speed of the discohesion, once started, defied all the belated efforts that were made to stop it—there are certain processes that are easy to start, but stopping them is like trying to gather grains of sand, one by one."

Kenlon was picturing the spread of the mud, the submerging of the land, the incoming tides sweeping over the dissolving continents; millions of living bodies must have sunk down to a choking death, into rivers and lakes and oceans of mud and water.

The visualization was so horrifying that it took several long moments for him to realize that, in spite of their planet almost literally liquifying under them, the human beings, before succumbing, had created the winged men and the fishmen.

And someone must have observed the villain of the piece. Because a winged man, returning to the past, had settled down with his time devices on the one and only ship in that time that was responsible.

It could not possibly have been a coincidence.

"Quite evidently," said the lizard being, "no other vessel of our people has ever come this way. So the duty devolves on us to settle this problem once and for all.

"Now, here is our offer.

"The fishmen are too much for us. We cannot possibly take over this planet so long as they exist.

"First, their city must be destroyed. Then they must be hunted down and killed to the last man. We can do the second part, but not the first.

"If you help us to do this, we shall make no effort to interfere with the life and activity of the winged men, and will of course harm no one else from the past, or place obstacles to their return to their own time.

"What is your decision?"

Kenlon didn't believe it.

They were a hundred years from their home planet, so they had to remain and solve the problem. This was their task, he deduced, from the horrifying story they had told. They had come looking for planets that could be converted into something ideal for their own race to live on; in earth, they had found such a planet and had converted it—and then, by some fantastic coincidence, they had been taken to the future by a winged man.

Here they were. Undoubtedly, they could journey home and come back with reinforcements, and proper equipment . . .

Kenlon's thought poised. "Why don't you do that?" he asked, after explaining his thought.

There was a pause; then, the being who had spoken turned and consulted with his fellows. There was a back and forth grunting and whistling with, however, no translation occurring.

Abruptly, the spokesman faced about and addressed Kenlon, and what he said now *was* translated.

"The journey there and back would require two hundred years. Meanwhile, the fishmen would achieve their purpose of destroying the winged men. But their real intent is to gain access to the computer memory in the eyrie. That holds secrets which would enable them to build thousands of cities like the one they now have."

He made a gesture that was not human at all. It was a body movement, a snakelike wiggle, an arching of a reptilian neck. What it meant was not obvious. Yet what the creature said was:

"So we have to stay and capture this planet now with what we have."

Kenlon persisted: "Well then, why don't you locate the computer in the eyrie and destroy it?"

Again the alien gesture. Kenlon decided that it was a body movement of dismissal of this suggestion.

"That computer," said the Yaz, "represents a science basically more advanced than ours, and it can defend itself from anything we've got."

"Can it defend itself from the fishmen?" Kenlon asked.

"It undoubtedly could, but if the winged men are defeated, it would regard itself as a servant of the other human race—the fishmen."

The lizard being broke off: "We assure you, Mr. Human Being, there is no alternative to the deal we offer. Your ship is necessary to our achieving our purpose; and so, here is our ultimatum—"

Ultimatum!

At some deep of his body, Kenlon felt a grisly fear, as that word was used.

"We shall," said the alien monster, "permit you to return to your ship—"

Kenlon felt a wave of terrible relief rush through him—terrible because of the feeling that remained that no matter what they did, he was their prisoner . . .

The lizard being continued:

"We shall allow you an indeterminate time to consider if there is any escape for you from what we want. You may consult with these other human beings, as you have already been doing. When a sufficient time has elapsed—in our estimation; days, weeks—which depends on your activity—we shall demand action from you. If you refuse, we shall begin to destroy these other ships, one by one, in the belief that this will put a pressure on you to agree. If it does not do so, we shall await an opportunity to seize your ship. Sooner or later, after you are alone—and have no other ships to help you—such an opportunity will occur. And now—

"You may go!"

Kenlon went.

Chapter 13

Later that morning:

"Somebody coming, sir!" was the message relayed from the deck to Kenlon. "The same people who were here yesterday."

Kenlon was astonished. "The Clen air carriage?" he wondered, as he headed up.

That *was* who it was. He stood on a deck that was slightly awash in a calm sea and watched the aircraft make its slow approach above the waves. After the extreme dullness of the morning, it had become another day in which clouds alternated with sunlight, each time bringing hint of more rain.

As he watched, he was presently able to recognize Dorilee. The closer the airship came, the more anxious he felt. He sensed purpose, and he remembered the desperation of these people. When they were a hundred yards away, he decided to take no chances but ordered everyone below and the hatches closed. His command was that the sub should crash dive at his signal.

After the threat of the Yaz, Kenlon did not believe that he was being too cautious. He suspected superior science on all those ships out there. He had the feeling that in some respects he and his crew were like spear-carrying savages confronted for the first time by rifles.

Minutes later, as Dorilee jumped smartly down on the submarine deck, he saluted her. She came forward and said in a formal tone, "The Sessa Clen has come to pay a visit to your ship."

Omigawd! thought Kenlon.

Aloud, he said, "You mean—she's aboard—she's along right now?"

"Yes. She's in the cabin below."

The feeling that came to Kenlon was a mixture of confusion, fear, desperation, and bafflement. The bafflement resulted from a strong conviction that the Sessa Clen would not even vaguely comprehend a refusal to let her come aboard. The desperation derived from his belief that, if she were to become angry with him, she could command an advanced science against him. And the fear was from his lifetime certainty that you couldn't reason with a genuinely feminine woman.

He had been tensely thinking of how he could mobilize all these people against the Yaz—the Clen yacht and its equipment would be of surpassing importance . . . His confusion at the woman's unexpected visit reflected his terrifying experience on the Yaz ship.

His tension evidently communicated to the big Joanna officer. A strained look came into Dorilee's face. "You're not thinking of refusing," she said, and there was a tremble in her voice. She broke off: "I couldn't take back a message like that. I'd have to kill myself."

Kenlon realized that in her situation she might well have no alternative.

"But what does she want?" he asked, in a helpless tone.

"She made up her mind when we watched you in the water last night," Dorilee said. "She couldn't believe that any man could be that brave. Men in the Clen era are"—she hesitated—"gentle."

She finished: "I think her visit is personal. She wants to have another look at you."

Kenlon was thinking wryly: The rain-filled night that had seemed so black to him and his men had apparently been like day to the advanced sciences of these others.

"Did you see those aboard?" he asked.

"No, there was a field blocking what was on and in the ship."

And still Kenlon temporized. "There's something I've

been wanting to ask you. You speak English perfectly without a translation machine. How do you do that?"

He finished distractedly, "And how do those translation machines work, anyway, that the others use?"

"We have a translation complex," Dorilee said, "but when we actually want to learn a language, we set up a field; and the language is imprinted directly onto the brain. Of course, it would be foolish to clutter the brain with the thousands of languages of history, so"—she shrugged—"when we need one, we imprint. When we're through with it, we de-imprint."

Kenlon was silent, startled.

The woman went on: "As for the translation machine itself, it took time to develop. It actually required a few lifetimes of study. But, once a master was in existence, there's always been that type of machine available."

As she described it, the languages of the world had early been broken down into their roots, then into their phonemes, and not only into the standard phonemes—pitch, sounds, inflections, stresses, and so on—but also into the sighs, rasps, breaths, and other audible behavior related to the spoken word.

As time passed, changes in the usage of, and combining of, these roots and phonemes were recorded—and were associated by the translation machine to all historical developments of the idea. The computer, upon "hearing" a language that it had not previously been programed for, scanned each word for its similarity to other phonemes and roots, related the most likely meaning, and so not only offered an instant translation of the strange language into one of the languages it "knew" but, as the new language continued to be spoken, examined each syllable for its many sounds, programed itself, and within moments was able to give simple, then progressively more complex answers in the language, with perfect colloquial pronunciation.

"You mean," said Kenlon, "these translators are not programed for English?"

"That is correct."

Kenlon remembered the slangy Americanese that Gand

had used with such facility, and he thought: "Well, I'll be damned!"

Something else occurred to him. "Has the Sessa had English imprinted on her brain for this visit?"

Dorilee's face took on a shocked expression. "Of course not," she said almost breathlessly. "It is inconceivable that any kind of energy field should be used on one of her rank."

"I presume she has similarly not been scientifically trained?" Kenlon said tensely.

"Of course not," said Dorilee indignantly.

It was the reassurance Kenlon had been somehow seeking while he temporized. He had doubted that the Sessa understood the science of her era. Now, he was convinced of it. He swallowed hard—and made his decision.

"Only the Sessa can come below," he said with finality.

Complete relief came into Dorilee's face. "Of course," she said.

She turned and hurried back to the air carriage. Kenlon hastily called Benjamin, Tedders, and several crew members to come on deck.

Tedders was calm, said nothing. But Benjamin was shocked. "You mean, you're actually going to let her go below?"

"Let me go first," said Kenlon, "then her, then you follow. Keep your hand on your gun."

"Yes, but how will I know if she makes a suspicious move? How do I decide that it's not right?"

It was a good question, but Kenlon had no time for it. "Just use your good sense," he said quickly. "After all, it's one woman against a hundred and twenty men. Here they come."

A set of steps had been lowered from the air carriage. Holding to the hand-hold of the steps perhaps a little more tightly than was necessary, the Sessa Clen walked daintily down to the metal runway.

Kenlon caught her hand as she stepped onto the swaying deck. A fairly strong sea was running, and the sub rolled with it in a manner to which she was evidently not accustomed; for she gasped and stopped and stood there, pale and visibly shaken.

But presently her lips tightened, and she started forward, holding his hand. She was a beautiful, regal-looking woman; and she followed Kenlon down into the interior. But when she reached the control room, something of her ladylike manner disappeared. Her eyes became bright and alert.

She spoke into a little wrist radio, and the translation came from Dorilee in the air carriage into a device fitted into Kenlon's ear:

"The Sessa is asking if the room where you are is the center from which all the automatic machinery is controlled?"

"That's right," said Kenlon.

The moment he had spoken, he realized that she had meant her question differently from his answer. To him, the control room was the center from which the commander directed the ship. Whereas automatic machinery and automatic controls implied something far more advanced.

In his daydreams he had sometimes tried to visualize a completely automatic submarine, requiring only one man to operate it. The use of the variable energy principle to control motor speeds, to control valves, to control the myriad functions aboard a sub should greatly reduce the normal hazards of submarining.

And then there were several dozen extensions of the gyroscope idea, already in use in various operations; and then there was . . .

The picture had never come quite clear. There were always a number of practical obstacles that his trained mind insisted on confronting. These obstacles rose up now to keep the picture he had tried to evoke as dim as ever.

Her words, and his thoughts about them, had another effect. They brought into new, vivid relief the fact that this woman was from a later age than his own. He felt suddenly breathless. He said, assuming Dorilee would reply, "You know, I've never asked you people what period of time you're from."

The Sessa Clen presently turned and looked at him. "The one hundred and thirty-fifth century after Christ," she said. Her words came through Dorilee's translation.

It was longer than he had thought. It alarmed him. The comparison that Kenlon made was with the people in the round ship from the Setidillad period. The Clen time was three thousand years after *that*. He vaguely visualized a scientific supremacy greater than he had imagined.

He thought, in fear: There's too much I don't know about these people.

As he glanced at the Sessa, uncertain as to what he should do, he saw that her hands were groping in the small, dainty handbag she carried. Her manner was diffident. She seemed to make up her mind, for she spoke firmly in her own language. Her hand came out of the bag, clutching a handful of white crystals.

In a single, spreading movement, she scattered them on the floor.

Actually, what happened then took place the instant the crystals came into view.

Something flowed from them, something palpable and strong that jangled his nerves. He heard a gasp from Benjamin. The officer seemed to freeze. Simultaneously, the assistant electrical engineering officer, who had been standing at attention beside the chart table chair, stiffened even more.

For a long moment, that was Kenlon's only awareness: the unpleasant tingling of his body, and his sight of the two rigid men.

The next second, Dorilee's voice translated what the blond Sessa had said: "By Clen law, a Sessa takes precedence over all other persons. By that law, I therefore take possession of this ship."

The words amazed Kenlon, and he was stimulated to make an effort.

Nothing happened.

He couldn't move. His muscles were held rigid by an unseen force.

With a desperate will, he fought to reach for his revolver. He couldn't move his hand.

The spasm of panic that surged through him was spurred by an awful sense of disaster. Vaguely, he was aware of Lieutenant Benjamin straining, tensing, in the same futile manner as himself.

He realized that the immobility extended to his fingers and to his face and throat, and to his legs and arms.

Kenlon stood as still as death, his mind pervaded with the knowledge that he was paralyzed.

A woman was about to capture a fully armed, fully manned United States submarine.

His confined world continued to be full of a number of things. The turbines chuttered away; there was the strong feel of the *Sea Serpent* rolling with the movement of the sea. Beyond the thick glass plates of the control room, in front of which the electrical engineering officer was standing, looking even more rigid now, the sea almost washed over the long deck. He saw his own men out there.

From the corner of one eye, Kenlon saw that Dorilee and another Joanna were coming down the steps from the air carriage. A few moments later, the two climbed into the control room. Dorilee remained. The Sessa and the second Joanna went up and out and onto the air carriage. Then Dorilee went below, with scarcely more than a look at him.

Kenlon stood there. He felt nothing, but his mind was clear. His body seemed normal. His heart must still be beating; his lungs performing their functions.

Yet he couldn't speak, couldn't move.

He presumed that the woman did not have any murderous intent. She was merely taking control of the submarine, in order to carry out the purpose of the winged men. All these people had discovered that the *Sea Serpent* alone could accomplish that purpose.

No matter what the limitation of her intention, it didn't make any difference. He was disgraced before his men. Within two days of inheriting command, he had lost the ship, and by the age-old method of a man being trapped by a woman.

After several minutes, he caught a flashing glimpse of Dorilee making her way toward the engine room and the stern torpedo room. She must have been forward sprinkling her damnable crystals. This very instant men were lying, or sitting, or standing, down there in whatever position paralysis had struck them—thinking about a commanding officer who had failed them.

Dorilee climbed up into the control room. She was carrying a heavy sack. "Hand guns," she explained.

"What a terrible ship," she went on, shuddering. "Everything so confined, and just a narrow corridor between those frightful engines."

Involuntarily, Kenlon's mind leaped back to the pigboats in which, as an officer in the naval reserve, he had taken his yearly training cruise. The brief wonder came, what would she have thought of those, compared to which the *Sea Serpent* was a luxury liner?

The thought snuffed out. He stood there. The expression on his face must have shown his strain. The woman glanced at him sharply.

"Stop it!" she said. "There's no disgrace in being defeated by superior science. I'm sure you're going to be sensible about this."

Kenlon knew that he wasn't. He had always recognized that women had a different psychological outlook from men. It took a woman to be completely oblivious to such dishonor as he had now suffered.

She was speaking again: "Ordinarily, we would never have taken such action as this. But the Sessa Clen's legal ascendency in this situation must be established."

Once more, grudgingly, Kenlon recognized that there was nothing basically evil here. He should have known, though, should have realized, that a woman on her way to be married was more of a human tigress than a human being.

"There is no reason," Dorilee said, "why there should be any bloodshed."

The statement was so odd that Kenlon was torn from his bitter meditation. The words seemed meaningless. Except for the two officers and the half-dozen men on the bridge, the ship was already lost.

Kenlon's mind poised there flooding with understanding. Tedders, Durosky, and the others. That was it. They had still to be disposed of; and there must be some difficulty about it.

"Those men outside," said the woman, "will either have to surrender or suffer serious injury. The neurals do not work in the open."

The "neurals" must be the paralyzing crystals. As for surrender—quite suddenly Kenlon knew that Tedders and the others were as good as dead.

It wasn't that Navy men never surrendered. But they would not yield immediately. And not, Kenlon was sure, to a woman. The thought collapsed as, out of the corner of his eye he saw the head and shoulders of Tedders bending over the open hatchway, heard Tedders say, "A winged man is coming sir; he—"

The words broke off. The officer roared: "What's going on down there?"

With a jerk, Tedders drew back, but his voice thundered down to Kenlon above the muffled sound of the turbines: "Durosky, all of you, grab your guns!"

He stepped onto the ladder, and the next moment his body came plunging down. He was followed by five men. It was beautifully fast work. Normally, it would have overwhelmed a single person. Now, they fell in a heap and lay rigid. The woman walked over and disentangled them. They sprawled stiffly, looking stupid, amazed, dismayed.

Kenlon saw that the woman was turning away from the fallen men, their guns gathered into the crook of her arm. She dumped the weapons into her sack, then drew a thin metal bar the size of a comb from her purse and approached Kenlon.

"I want you to go up on deck and persuade your junior officer to be rational. You will be able to do this because this charged plate"—she held up the bar—"will release you from thrall about a minute after I put it into your hand."

She thrust it downward toward him. Kenlon felt the coolness of it against his hand; he hadn't, until it touched his skin, realized how feverish he was. The coolness was like a breath of air blowing into a hot, dry room.

"As soon as you are able," said the Tenant, "close your fingers around it. And don't do anything rash. I can neutralize the bar in a flash."

He didn't believe that. Her own immunity must derive from something like this; and if she neutralized his, then she too would be subject to the neurals. In spite of this conviction, he had no intention of testing her statement by counteraction until he could figure out a plan.

This whole thing had to be thought out, perhaps even argued out, before action could be wisely taken. There was a second winged man outside now. If he could manage to tell him the state of affairs, and persuade him that the whole purpose of the winged men was endangered by this highhanded seizure . . .

The thought drained away. Quite automatically he had flexed his fingers, and they moved. And, strangely, just like that, the awful depression of spirits left him. He clutched the bar convulsively, and watched the woman back away, her gaze narrowed on his face, one of her hands resting lightly on a metal rod at her belt. She said:

"As soon as you have talked to your man on deck, I shall give you some clothing, which has the neutralizing element woven into the fabric. You can wear it under your uniform. There is no reason why you should be under restraint. We have no desire to cause unnecessary indignity to anyone on this vessel."

"You're making a grave mistake," Kenlon said. "You can't possibly operate this submarine without its trained crew. You—"

He stopped. Speech had come so naturally that it took a moment to realize that only seconds before his vocal cords had been paralyzed. He lifted his arm, then took a step; and it was all easy and natural again. He was free.

He said in an unsteady voice, "I urge you to give us back possession. I promise to hold a meeting with everybody on this matter of an attack against the fishmen. You'll get nowhere by the course you're pursuing."

"You had better hurry on deck," the Joanna said grimly. "The situation there can't be improving."

It wasn't. A pale Durosky had his gun trained on the air carriage, and he was waving threateningly at those aboard.

The uniformed Joannas crouched behind their gunwale, aiming a long metal rod at Durosky. The Sessa was nowhere visible; she must have gone to her stateroom. Durosky listened to Kenlon's explanation of what had happened, got a blank expression on his face, and said finally:

"What am I supposed to do, sir—leave the gun?"

The question shook Kenlon. A little unsteadily, he walked over to the hatch and called down to the woman:

"You still insist on going through with this?"

"Tell your man," came the clear, firm answer, "to get away from the gun. Then invite my Joannas aboard."

Slowly, Kenlon straightened. He felt old and tired. He stared almost unseeingly out to the gray sea, then up to the mountain in the sky, the lower end of which sagged a third of a mile above him.

The half blank upward glance brought into his view the winged man whom Tedders had reported. The flying man was circling about three hundred feet up, peering down at the scene. He seemed uncertain; his movements lacked purpose. The very aimlessness ended the slim hope that he might bring the help that was needed within seconds. Kenlon sighed and turned to his junior.

"All right, Durosky," he said, "come out of there."

A moment later, the Joannas were briskly jumping aboard. Resistance was at an end.

Chapter 14

There was not much physical change in his position. Kenlon wandered disconsolately to the railing and stared forward. In a vague way, he was aware of the air carriage drifting slowly away from the *Sea Serpent,* one lone Joanna in it. Obviously, she was taking the Sessa back to the parent ship.

He was aware, too, that, of the five Joannas who had come aboard, four went below, leaving one to guard Durosky and himself. One woman to look after two men. Kenlon laughed curtly. In view of the fact that a single female had conquered a ship with a crew of over a hundred, the one guard, in the truest meaning of relative values, actually outnumbered them by about twenty to one.

His reverie ended as Durosky put his right elbow on the railing, then lowered his weight onto the elbow. The older man sallied gloomily:

"Is big sister going to tuck us below too, where we'll be out of the way?"

Kenlon groaned: "She plans to save me from indignity by letting me walk around clutching this metal bar." He lifted his hand and the bar with a vague gesture, then went on: "I can learn to grin like an ape and that way maybe I can administer good cheer to the men.

"It might be the only way," he added hopefully, "of getting them out from under the spell of the crystals. One look at me, I mean, and they'd have to get up and punch my face. It would be irresistible."

"Frankly," Durosky said soberly, "that doesn't sound as if it will work, though I'd be willing to add my mug as a specially seductive punching bag." He added, "What do you think those neurals are made of?"

Kenlon described briefly the feeling of energy flow that had impinged on his body. "I would say the crystals give off electrical impulses that interfere with those nerves which attempt to carry out voluntary actions on impulse or command from the brain." He went on grimly: "I have some lunatic notion of waiting for an opportune moment, and then going around and sweeping up all the crystals and tossing them overboard."

Durosky said, "You won't pull anything like that on little Dorilee. That woman reminds me of my father's second wife."

"I suppose," said Kenlon, "we'll just have to accept the situation. I believe she will hand the ship back to us afterward. My duty, therefore, is to ease the minds of the men, and do everything possible to see that these Joannas don't wreck the sub. I can't let a hundred and twenty men down, or take risks with our sub, because my pride is hurt."

It was a dismal solution. But Kenlon had arrived at it during the anguished moments before surrender; and every minute that passed made it seem more practical.

"Personally," he said harshly, "I hate the fishmen for the ruthlessness of their action against the skipper. It was a cold-blooded business, treating us as if we were so many subhuman beasts. But I never thought it a strong enough reason to destroy their city, particularly as I had in mind something that's never been mentioned: The groundmen, the mighty groundmen, who made both the winged men and the fishmen, created two types for a purpose, nothing less than that man should continue to exist on Earth in spite of the greatest catastrophe that surely has ever befallen an inhabited planet.

"To undermine that plan, that great purpose, to satisfy the desire of this Clen woman to get married is the most pitiful excuse for action that I've ever heard.

"I'm willing to admit," Kenlon went on less violently, "that frightful flaws may have occurred in the two species who were made to carry out this plan. The fishmen *seem* to be at fault, and to be the aggressors—Nemmo tells me they've got tractor beams on the floor of the sea under here, and have already drawn the sky island a mile downward to the water. Their intention is to submerge it, and drown all the winged men; so Nemmo tells me. If that's true, then something drastic should be done to stop them. But there are complications." He meant the Yaz, yet dared not say so, for they would be watching him and would be in favor of what the Joannas wanted. He finished uneasily: "If these Clen actually succeed in destroying the fishmen's city, that could be the end of man on Earth. They—"

He stopped, because he saw the Tenant come on deck. The woman spoke to the Joanna guard.

"Wave that winged man down," she said. "He should have been able to see by this time that the capture was successfully carried out."

Kenlon had the feeling that he had not heard right. He turned, his whole body stiff. "What did you say?" he asked in a flat voice. "The winged men are party to this assault?"

He didn't need the affirmative answer she gave. The Joanna had beckoned. And in response the winged thing in the sky was growing second by second in size.

Funny that he had not during the whole period, while the *Sea Serpent* was being captured, thought of the winged men as having a pre-connection. It all fitted, of course. In their desperation, they had very cunningly used the Sessa Clen's anxiety to occupy her marriage bed. Their desperation must be great indeed to have overridden the gentle racial character traits he had discovered in Nemmo.

Kenlon felt a sudden sadness. The whole business was becoming more sordid every minute. But though there now seemed no alternative, he refused to accept it as the end.

The winged man's gingerly extended, gray-clothed feet touched the railing. Lightly, the man wafted down beside Kenlon. He was a little taller than Nemmo, and younger, more personable. His face, however, had the same hawk-

like qualities; thinness, blazing gray-blue eyes. He wore
the same furry cloth from the neck down, which fitted
so snugly that, as in Nemmo's case, it was hard to believe that it was not part of his body. His wings were a
very dark gray, with here and there streaks of black. He
walked over to Dorilee without looking at Kenlon.

"Any trouble?" he asked in his own language.

"Naturally not!" was the tart response.

Kenlon smiled grimly. It would be nice to be so positive. Not that she wasn't telling the truth. There hadn't
been any trouble worth mentioning.

He liked her less and less.

The winged man was speaking. "There is a change in
the plans."

"Change?" said Dorilee. Before the man could answer,
she went on snappingly: "All you've got to do, Laren, is
tell us where the undersea city is. We'll do the rest."

"The council," said Laren, "wants to see him first."

"The council!" said Dorille. "The council. That's all I
ever hear. First, the council advises you not to tell us the
location of the city; and you don't tell us. Then—"

She paused, scowling. She lost all claim to prettiness
when she scowled. "I thought," she finished, "you winged
men were ignoring the council in this."

Laren shook his head. He said with a quiet dignity:
"We shall never ignore the council. It distresses us that, in
this affair, its ancient purposes seem to be clashing with
the harsh reality of our situation."

He broke off: "I see no reason why Commander Kenlon should not be taken before the council. You will need
time to familiarize yourself with the undersea craft.
Nemmo will remain aboard to give you any assistance he
may be capable of."

Dorilee laughed. It was a hard laugh. The sound of it
brought the thought to Kenlon, that victory did not add
any grace to her character. She said arrogantly:

"I do not anticipate any difficulty in operating the submarine. The commander here, and his crew, have a far
more important interest in seeing that nothing goes wrong
than I have. Their ship is at stake."

She finished indifferently: "But you can have him for a while if you want him. I have sent for a technical book about ancient submarines, and naturally we shall familiarize ourselves with the machinery. Don't let the council keep him too long."

There was a curious, resentful look on Laren's face. It was obvious that he didn't like her casual contempt for the council. When he spoke, it was on that subject still. He said:

"We have no desire to do without the wisdom of the council. Perhaps it will give him some information useful in the attack. We *know* that it will do nothing harmful to our interests."

He seemed to realize that his words were being wasted. He turned to Kenlon. "I hope you will not object to coming to our city."

Kenlon did not reply immediately. He had been following the give-and-take of the conversation with a gathering blankness. Memory of what Nemmo had said about the council merely served now to add to his confusion.

The general picture was clear enough. The council of the winged men had released the information that made possible construction of the time tubes which were used to bring the submarine and other craft to A.D. 24,999. Yet the council opposed the action to be taken by the seized ships. To this opposition the winged men were paying no attention.

It was clear but queer.

Laren was speaking again. "You cannot imagine, Commander, how much we regret the tactics we have been forced to use. It is against all our instincts. I hope, sir, you will come up and see the council."

Kenlon had not intended to give the impression that he was refusing. Of all the things he wanted most was more knowledge—about everything that was going on. He turned to Dorilee, said:

"Before I go, Tenant, I hope you won't mind if I take a few precautions to protect my vessel."

"You may be sure," said Dorilee, "that anything within

reason along those lines will have my support. I realize the danger from the fishmen."

Not only from the fishmen—Kenlon thought grimly. There was another sea creature to be wary of: the Yaz beings.

Kenlon bowed a stiff acknowledgment, then explained to Laren what Nemmo had said about the Gihlander protective lamps, adding:

"My idea is that you detach your time machines"—he pointed—"from our nose and stern, and lower them, lighted up, into the water. Their penetrative powers are so great that they should make all the water for a considerable distance literally transparent. The Joanna guards can keep watch. That way we can shut off the engines."

He saw, even before he finished, that Laren was smiling.

"The Gihlander lamps," the winged man explained, "are ideal for the purpose you describe. They give an enormous light, but have no dangerous properties." He smiled again, finished: "I have allowed this conversation to be overheard at our communications center, so it shouldn't take long for the carriers to arrive."

Kenlon had been wondering how he was going to be transported. The answer began to be clear when he saw more than two score winged men wheeling down from the sky. They brought the lamps. They also brought a sling—supported by scores of thin wires, each one of which was attached to the belt around the waists of the flyers.

After everything else had been done, Kenlon climbed into the sling; and in a minute his feet left the deck, and he was on his way.

He was looking down at the conning tower and the long, bulging shape of the submarine floating like a toy in bright, transparent water. The glow points of the Gihlander lamps, which hung now in the water, curiously accentuated the impression of a toy submarine in an indoor pool with ceiling lights reflecting from the water.

Kenlon swung slowly around and around in his harness and swayed gently from side to side. To his left he could see the gleaming metallic shapes of the various vessels—Gand's big ship, the Sessa Clen's yacht.

The ships receded slowly. The sea took on a flat appearance. The wall of the eyrie loomed black and near to one side, and below and above, blocking out three quarters of his view in the direction the submarine's instruments had always indicated as being west.

After a few minutes more, the *Segomay 8* disappeared behind an outjutting angle of the mountain, and one by one, as he watched, the other craft were blotted from his view until, finally, only the speck that was the *Sea Serpent*, and the high-riding, red-glinting ship of the Sessa Clen, remained in his field of vision.

Kenlon estimated that he was at least a mile above the sea. Which left about half a mile to go, before he reached the building. He glanced upward to verify the distance, and it was so.

Laren must have noticed the intent expression that Kenlon always got in his face when he calculated. He winged down to a point just below Kenlon. He called melodiously:

"Anything wrong?"

Kenlon started to shake his head; and then with a jerk that was as much physical as mental, stopped the action. Anything wrong! Everything was wrong, his whole universe topsy-turvy. Of all the things in the world that he needed, more information was the most important. Information that would straighten out the bends in his mind. Information that would fill enormous gaps. *Information!* First, about the council.

He stated his confusion, finished: "What I want to know is, why is the council opposed?"

Laren said gravely: "It would take too long to explain the council to you. Theoretically, it is omniscient. We are disturbed by its reactions to this affair. You will realize the difficulty of our problem in a few minutes when you see the council."

Kenlon considered that, frowning. An omniscient council whose findings had to be overruled—it was puzzling. He twisted toward Laren. "Why didn't you," he began, "send someone to the age of the last groundmen with your problem? Better than any twentieth-century submarine, they'd be able—"

He was talking to empty air. Laren, evidently taking his brief silence for the end of the conversation was swinging strongly upward a hundred feet away.

Kenlon thought of beckoning him back but, after a moment's consideration, changed his mind. Knowing what he knew—through what he had learned of Arpo's character—of the great groundmen, it seemed obvious that the council had understood the situation very well. Being totally altruistic, they had given their help at the time. They would not take sides.

And so—Kenlon reasoned—he had better start thinking about what he was going to ask the omniscient council.

He was still frowningly preparing his questions a few minutes later when he grew aware that the flight was leveling off. And that he had come to the end of his aerial journey.

Chapter 15

They were not, Kenlon saw, at the top of the building, but about halfway up. An open door, a very large door, at least a hundred feet wide and high, yawned directly before him. Marble steps led down from it and terminated in space.

It was one of many such entrances in a building the grand dimensions of which were only now apparent. It towered and spread. It was wider than it was high. But it was *high*. It floated in clouds; part of it was hidden in thick mists. He could see the remote upper reaches through shimmering fog. And those heights were at least an eighth of a mile farther up.

The building in itself was a city.

Everywhere he looked were winged men and women, in groups and singly, though none was near the door toward which he was being edged. Kenlon gazed in fascination at the women, though they were mostly too far away for him to make them out clearly.

Of the two nearest him, one had jet black hair, the other golden. The hair was very long and whipped behind them as they flew. Kenlon thought of angels, but he was vaguely glad that they came no closer. He had, he thought as his feet settled on the comfortingly hard marble terrace, no fancy for disillusionments.

"Just walk in, but go carefully," said Laren.

Evidently, he was to remain in his harness, attached to the fliers. The precaution evoked a mind picture of what the inside must be like. Kenlon walked gingerly through the doorway.

He found himself in a well-lighted and vast room.

There were great unguarded holes in the floor, in the ceiling, in the walls; gleaming tunnels that fell away into depths, or gave tantalizing glimpses of tastefully furnished antechambers to what must be apartments because there were closed doors visible in some of the horizontal vistas along which Kenlon gazed.

Height untrammeled by too many walls—that was the general effect. Kenlon, his neck arched, his whole manner one of a gaping tourist, walked forward until he felt Laren's withholding pressure on his arm. Startled, he looked down—at an abyss of a tunnel unguarded by rails of any description. The floor actually curved down, so that there was no sharp edge. Beyond the curving floor was a gulf forty feet wide and three-quarters of a mile deep. Kenlon reeled back, and then flushed as, beside him, Laren laughed softly.

The winged man said, "Have no fear. The carriers could support you even in a sudden fall. You realize, of course, that in a world where men have wings living quarters will be different."

Kenlon realized silently.

Laren went on: "You are to be taken down about—" He gave the winged men's equivalent of a hundred meters. He finished with an enigmatic smile: "Do not be too surprised at the nature of the council."

Before Kenlon could reply, Laren launched himself down the shaft. The sling tightened around Kenlon. He was swung out and down. Below him, he saw Laren land, and stand, looking up. An intervening ceiling hid the council room; then he could see more of the floor beyond Laren. And then ...

He was flying.

He was flying. There was no mistaking the movement, the free, the immensely strong, movement. He was flying through a thick mist of cloud that hid even the tips of his wings.

His vision included eye awareness of his legs drawn up against his body; and it included blurred visualization of his wings—blurred because the two great pinions were hammering away at the air like the pistons of a swiftly running engine. His body glowed with power; his whole being exulted with the glory of winged flight. The exhilaration was a tingling joy inside him.

For a long minute that was all there was. Then slowly his mind began to emerge from the state of rigidity into which it seemed to have frozen. The period of pure impression ended. And a personal thought was born, the first of many. A thought so powerful, so devastating, that his wings ceased their pumping, his body twisted with amazement; he felt bewildered, stunned. And still that thought would not be eased, but rather grew like a storm, becoming more intense with each passing moment:

What—*what*—*WHAT* had happened?

The winged men had been lowering him toward the council room; the floor of the room was actually coming into his view when—*this!*

Flying. With wings. Actually inside—his brain, his consciousness, his being inside the body of a winged man.

They must have done it on purpose. They must have transferred his—essence—into the body of this winged man in order to show him the mental and physical universe of the race.

Kenlon clung to that logicalization even as awareness came that he was flying again. Without having consciously willed it, he was climbing strongly upward toward whatever high goal the winged man, into whose body he had been transferred in mid-flight, had been originally heading.

He felt a sudden, intense curiosity as to that goal. He fought on up through the incredible cloud formation, up, up. His wings were soaking wet, but their strength defied the clinging water. The great heart, the mighty lungs, the untiring muscles of the body he bore, accepted every ounce of that terrific strain, and still they climbed.

Kenlon's mind grew immensely weary of that struggle against gravity and the resisting elements; and it was then that he became aware that it was not *he* who was doing the flying.

He tried to stop the wings in their flapping. And

couldn't. He tried to end that upward flight, and twist downward—and couldn't!

Dismayed, he ceased the effort. He thought blankly: I'm just a rider. The brain of the real winged man is still here, still in charge. I'm being shown. I'm not participating. But then, what about the way he had stopped the wings from movement earlier?

The answer came to him instantly: The violence of his reaction at the moment of discovering his predicament had succeeded in dominating the nerves and muscles of the winged man. But only for that one shocked moment. There must be liaison; he must be capable of potential half-control. But it would require a desperate impulse to enforce it.

He had better remain quiet and await events.

The decision was barely made when the all-enveloping mist began to clear. First he could see the tips of his wings, then the beginning of a second pair of wings, then all around him other wings beating at the thinning air, mounting up now through ever fleecier clouds.

Abruptly, they burst into sunlight, climbed several hundred yards, and leveled off.

Whatever the purpose of it, the tremendous climb was over.

Their purpose could, of course, be to see the sun. It was reason enough. A month of gray skies had filled Kenlon with a longing to bask in pure, unadulterated sunlight.

If he felt thus, what then must these winged ones feel, whose horizon was always hidden by fog and mist and cloud?

He watched them experiencing the reality of the sun.

For a while they simply floated, wings almost moveless. They seemed to be resting on the great ocean of atmosphere beneath them, with only an occasional shunting of a wing to take advantage of the air that breathed now this way, now that. Silence lay over that high world. There was a grand dignity about it all, a sense of the spirit ascendant over the strife far below.

Here in this sky loft was peace enough to soothe any soul. The sun shone in a deep blue sky, a glorious orb of fire in an azure transparency. And there was no feeling of chill, though that could have been because the gray clothes fitted so snugly around each body.

There were at least two hundred bodies. They kept gliding in and out, one among the others, so that an accurate count was impossible. Kenlon judged that half of them were women.

Watching the women, the way their long hair streamed behind them, he thought again of angels; and this time he could see that the description was almost accurate. They were smaller than the men. Their faces were delicate, finely molded, their hands lovely, somehow untouched by the crude ardor of the wind and the perpetual dampness of the mists below.

It was the women who started the singing. Their voices intruded gently upon the silence, as if first one, and then others, following some secret cue, joined the swelling chorus.

Clear as running water, their voices ran the gamut of a song that was at once unbearably sweet yet tuneless, without coherent rhythm or pattern. A universe of sadness and joy quavered in their tones and semitones.

The men took up the words, and now, Kenlon saw, the whole group was flying and singing in unison.

Their song seemed the very essence of the music of an old and gentle race to whom tragedy had come. After a little, Kenlon was able to make out the meaning of the words, though he caught only snatches of the words themselves. Like the music, the words had no rhyme, no meter; and they did not even seem to be broken into verses:

> We are the winged.
> We sing of ancient glories and of a world to be.
> When the water is gone, and there is land again
> To hold our eager feet.
> For a 999 of three-ones we have kept our faith
>   with destiny.
> We have borne children to carry on the race of
>   men.
> Their children have borne children.

We have lived as the council advised.
Now we are threatened.
The men of the sea envy us our wings.
They desire to bring us low;
And we have no weapons.
We have no material from which to build
  weapons.
We have only the council, which tells us to be
  brave,
And to carry on in faith and hope for the future.
We have faith and hope in the future,
But we are disturbed; we feel there is need for
  strong action.
For a 999 of three-ones we must live our life;
A 999 of three-ones of waiting, of marking time,
  of simply living until Earth once more is a
  green paradise.
Then we will put aside our wings
And go to work.
It will be hard,
For we are the winged.

It was a hymn to the First Cause of the infinite, half longing appeal, half gratitude for existing joys. The song died as it had begun, gradually, until finally only a single crystal-clear woman's voice sustained a note, that faded into silence.

The group were flying swiftly now, in ranks of nines. They wove intricately in and out in a sort of winged dance. Faster, faster—spinning, diving, looping, always, fantastically always, in perfect timing. The maneuver was a hundred times more complicated than any earthly dance, its movements three dimensional, its purpose somehow symbolical of the song that had gone before. Sad with longing, sweet with past joys, tinged with the uncertainty of the present, it ended finally as each group of nine joined into a series of circles around a central group of nine. They hovered there.

A man began a discourse in a grave, gentle yet resonant voice:

"On this day we shall discuss the history of the spiritual development of the mighty groundmen, as revealed by the known sages in the last nine years before the catstrophe. Let no one doubt but that mankind attained its spiritual zenith in those dark, brave days, and that in the face of final disaster their true greatness was revealed as never before in the history of this aged Earth of ours. We—"

The voice faded strangely away from Kenlon. The scene dimmed, and withdrew, and then winked out.

The next instant he was swimming.

Chapter 16

The water was warm; that was all he knew at first. It was hard to see, mainly, Kenlon realized after a long, blank moment, because the body he was in wasn't paying particular attention to surroundings.

Awareness came that there was a strong current running. And that he was idling along in its grasp, with only an occasional plunge of his great arm or leg to aid his swift passage. He caught a glimpse of the bottom fifty feet below; and there was light filtering in from about an equal distance above. A dozen man-shapes were swimming near him in the dim reaches of water. He was one of a group of fishmen swimming in a shallow sea perhaps near a shore.

Kenlon's mind reached out to grasp the wider, greater implications. And they came clear and stunning. He was being shown. The fairness of it was absolutely staggering. First, the life and life-purposes of the winged men, now the fishmen.

The water was delightfully warm; and it billowed gently in and out of his gills, in and out, in and out. The action was as natural as all the breathing he had ever done. Kenlon was aware of it only because he concentrated *his* mind on it in a sudden fascination with the very idea of a human being swimming under water like a fish. After a minute the reality was too normal to think about. It was a part of life, like the steady beating of a strong heart, like the quiet action of a stomach during the process of digestion.

He forgot about it.

His interest turned to what was happening. Wonder

119

came as to where these water people were heading. He had an impression of alert attention to something going on in the sea darkness some distance in front of them.

The realization was like a cue. From out of the night of water came a thrillingly strange cry. It was a human voice, but unlike anything Kenlon had ever heard, a sound molded by the water environment, wonderfully alive, lusty in its piercing quality. Incredibly, though it was in an extremely modified version of the language of the winged men, he understood every syllable.

It was a warning.

"It's coming!" the voice cried. *"Prepare!"*

He felt himself patting the long knife in the sheath at his side. There was a darkly gleaming flash in the darkness ahead. A fish, Kenlon saw; a big fish. Twenty feet long at least. A shark! This was a hunting party.

A strong, big arrogant fish. It swam into plain view, seemed to pause as it saw the semicircle of shapes waiting for it, then disdainfully darted up approximately between Kenlon's body and that of the fishman next to him.

Faster than the shark, the fishmen plunged upward. And they had it. Kenlon's arm closed with a viselike strength around the thick, sturdy body, directly in front of the sinister triangulated fin on the hard back. His long knife slid with beautiful precision into the soft white belly.

Other knives were darting their death thrusts. The mad threshings ceased finally. The wild beast of the sea turned lazily over, and lay motionless in death.

No, not motionless. It yielded to the pressure of the current, and began to drift swiftly back the way it had come. Kenlon climbed on top of it, jackknifed his legs around its body, and sat casually while it floated into the darkness. In a few seconds, his companions were nowhere to be seen. He was alone with the dead fish, drifting toward an unknown destination.

The darkness did not last long. He grew aware of a glimmer in the distance. For a moment, a curious moment, Kenlon thought he had gotten his up and sideways directions mixed, and that it was the sun ahead there. The illusion ended as the shimmering glow widened, and spread into a vast expanse of light.

The city under the sea drew majestically into view.

It was impossible to obtain a good look. To the individual, whose body he shared, all this was completely unmarvelous; the man simply didn't notice. He began to paddle vigorously, as they approached the city. That restricted Kenlon's examination even more. Because his body was intent on the task of breaking free of the current that gripped him and the dead shark.

He made it, apparently with absolutely accurate results, because a minute later he had shoved the shark into a water lock inside the transparent wall of the city and climbed in after it. The lock door slid shut; a pump began to work silently. The instant the water was gone, an inner door opened; and Kenlon stepped briskly through it. He was in the city under the sea.

Kenlon had a conviction that he should feel some tremendous emotion. To be inside the city of the fishmen, he thought, actually inside. To be here to see and examine and judge. After a second, there was still no great surge of feeling along his nerves. Memory came of how calmly he had taken the fantastic experience of being in the body of a winged man—after the first shock.

It was clear that emotions in these detached states were on a stabler plane. It all seemed to work on the basis of a tiny percentage of what it would have been in his own body. He was an Olympian spectator aware of and influenced, but not maddened, by his observations.

Being inside the city meant no more to Kenlon's companion mind then being out. But that very fact now worked in Kenlon's favor. The fishman stood without interest, his mind apparently concentrated on some inner problem, his gaze absently studying the city. Kenlon had time to observe the main pattern.

The sea city, he decided, was roughly shaped like an enormous igloo. Inside it were a series of ten other igloos, each one progressively smaller by about the radius of a city block than the one before it. It was an immensely strong and clever arrangement. If the outer wall were breached by the corroding sea, then the second layer would take the stupendous load with the same fervor of resistance.

What was more, only a very small section of each layer could ever be flooded at one time, since the layers were divided into sections and floors. He was standing high up, looking down into geometrical arrays of lights and floors that extended into distance.

Everywhere were people working. Giants bending over machines that pulled loads—doing a thousand tasks, the nature of which was hidden from Kenlon, mostly by distance, but partly by the disinterest of his body.

Abruptly, the latter reason became dominant. His body ceased its inactive contemplation and walked rapidly toward a pile of almost flat metal sheets that, as he came up to them, showed themselves to be not metal. Kenlon stepped onto the topmost sheet, and, bending down, touched a button he hadn't noticed until the action was taken. The sheet rose up from the floor, and wafted over to the air lock. Kenlon's large fingers pressed the button again; and the shark was *drawn* up from where it lay in the lock and deposited onto the carrier.

Shark and Kenlon and carrier flowed off at speed down inclined floors toward the lower depths of the city. Kenlon had fleeting glimpses of fishmen working metal at machines, fishmen in laboratories that glittered with machinery. Each large room had in it a pillar of light that looked like nothing Kenlon had ever seen before.

Fishmen working—that was the general picture. Not singing, not dancing, but working. Here was a busy civilization in the making. Human beings with gills, living a savage, semiprimitive existence in a city built by men with whom they had no more in common than the winged men who had been spawned in the same terrible hour for the same basic purpose.

Beyond all doubt, the fishmen were trying to make something of their environment. They were fitting into it, *using* it rather than yielding to it. In them, the unconquerable spirit of man was manifesting in all its immense and variegated forms, whereas the winged men . . .

Kenlon shook himself mentally. He felt uneasy. The comparison was unfair. The winged men had no alternative, no opportunity. They could not but live for the future. And what was more, the lust of the fishmen to destroy the flying men was absolutely inexcusable. It was aggression with a capital A, murder-intent of the worst kind because the victims had no weapons, no defense. The moment their sky structure was completely under water, the winged people, with nowhere to land, would drown to the last man, woman and child.

Such a fate shared simultaneously by 239,999 human beings, an entire race, was so frightful that . . . He refused to contemplate it.

But if the alternative was the destruction of the stronger race, what then?

Kenlon did a mental equivalent of sighing. He was beginning to see the immensity of the human problem of this remote age.

The journey ended abruptly in a room that contained nothing but a great metal machine. It was metal this time, identifiable at close range. The machine had no attendant; there was no sound of movement from it, nor sign; no activity that affected any of the senses.

The powerful hand of Kenlon's body touched a lever. A hole gaped in the machine. Into this the shark was drawn by the same invisible power that had originally deposited it on the thin, sheetlike carrier.

The covering glided down on the hole. Kenlon's body stepped off the carrier and walked rapidly to a nearby door. Its mind seemed uninterested in the fate of the shark, and, after a little, Kenlon pushed it to a far part of his attention, also.

He was being shown a part of a day's—or whatever they called a time period—activities of one fishman. No portion of those activities mattered particularly. The shark was an incident; so was the present brisk walk. What was interesting was: What next?

He had a feeling that this incarnation was almost due

to end. But after at least ten minutes he was still there, still watching the unfolding life of a fishman.

The man carried on conversations but these made sense only in their total effect; the particular sentences and words added mood and fragment, but meant little in themselves.

There was a brief bit, carried on with a chance-met fellow fishman, that went:

"Hail!" said Kenlon's body. "How go the statistics?"

"Deplorably, Getta."

"How many recalcitrants this period?"

"Total, 1,111,999. That doesn't include the unknowns born at sea during the last ten generations, and never registered."

"I mean, how many new ones."

"83,999."

"Our birth rate is greater than that. But I can see your point. The call of the sea is becoming stronger. How many strangers registered?"

"999."

"So few! Hm-m-m!"

They walked on.

Another conversation—with a woman this time, a handsome giantess, who began:

"I'm just up from the mines, Getta. They need help down there."

"I shall pass on the information," Getta responded sardonically. "My own inclinations do not run to grubbing in the earth."

"You men!" said the woman reproachfully. "Always out in the water."

"Mouth breathing is unpleasantly dry and unwholesome."

"That's only your imagination. You were made to breathe in air and water equally well. It's the mystery, the wildness of the sea, not the breathing."

"It's something," Getta acknowledged. "Why not go with me. I'll guarantee you a dozen men."

The woman laughed. "The law that a woman who becomes a recalcitrant cannot return to the city is enough

for most of us women. I love the city as much as the sea.
I wouldn't care to be barred from either."

"If you change your mind," said Getta, "let me know."

They went their separate ways. Another conversation
was with a man.

"Whither bound, Getta?"

"To the eastern gate. You know my skill with the water
swallowers?"

"I have heard of it."

"It is very important that a revival be accomplished; so
says the council."

"Are we still consulting the council on matters of pol-
icy? I thought it was used only as a source of science information."

"We consulted it this time. Of course it happened that
our general opinion tended the same way."

"Well, good luck."

"Thanks."

It was not long afterward that Getta-Kenlon arrived at
what Kenlon surmised was the eastern gate. There was a
lock there similar to the one through which the shark had
been originally brought.

After five minutes, something moved in the sea outside.
Three bodies, swimming close together. They surged into
the lock, and the water turned whitish as it drained out.
The inner door slid open—and Getta faced it for the first
time. Two giants emerged, carrying the limp body of
Jones-Gordon. One of them said:

"Well, here he is, Getta. Shouldn't be too hard to revive. Swallowed only a little water before we sealed him
up—"

For Kenlon, the words blurred. Darkness, like an im-
penetrable mask, engulfed his senses.

Chapter 17

He could think. There was no sound, no feeling, no taste, no smell, no sight. But his brain worked. It was a trembling world of thought in which he found himself, because the thought itself seemed too big for his brain, the thought that . . .

The skipper was alive.

Or rather would be alive as soon as he had been resuscitated by Getta, the expert at reviving water swallowers. Getta's was probably more than just a human capability. The medical science he worked with must be very advanced.

Alive . . . Jones-Gordon . . .

In the darkness, Kenlon's mind writhed in a torment of reaction—and accepted the mighty fact. It was as if someone had been waiting for him to reach that conclusion. A voice spoke to him.

No, not spoke. For there was no sound, yet there was meaning, outside words impinging on his brain. No flat monologue was that bodiless, soundless voice. It was alive with overtones. It glowed. Richness pervaded every syllable that had meaning.

The voice said:

"Lieutenant Kenlon, you have seen. Now you must decide.

"The threat to the men who fly is real and terrible. Because it is rooted deep in the logic of human nature, in this case the logic of the men of the sea, who with remorseless rationalization believe that the two races cannot live together when there is land again.

"Coldly ruthless, they realize that it is easier to destroy

126

now 239,999 winged men than it will be to destroy 999 times that number who will be reproducing in their multiple nine-ones when the land is free again. Such is the argument of the seamen.

"In their turn, the winged men have come to feel that only the destruction of the sea city will save them.

"You must choose between them, you must decide. Now, are there any questions?"

Kenlon struggled. In a mental sweat, he fought to bring forth a sound out of the darkness that held him, one tiny sound that would release his voice to rattle out the questions in his mind.

No sound came. But the questions throbbed, and filled his mental world—and suddenly the answers came, one by swift one:

"The Yaz are unquestionably a problem.

"Yes, although it was already too late, they were identified as being the destroyers of the continents.

"No attempt was made to harm them, of course, first because the great groundmen did not think in such terms, and second because any intelligent life is better than none. The Yaz are still oriented to race ideas and can only conceive of a universe fitted to their own needs.

"As one of two surviving councils, I was given the information about the Yaz that motivated me to have their ship brought to this scene.

"Therefore you may realize that whatever decision is achieved here will be final for man and life on this planet.

"Unquestionably, in time the Yaz can search the sea shallows for all those fishmen who have left their city. But that is a task for their future.

"Yes, the fishmen, too, have a council. It is located in the central core of their city. Unfortunately, they use it mostly as a library, and seldom ask its advice. Such is ever the way of strong, youthful races.

"Your commander is even now alive.

"It is impossible to use the time tubes to go for help into the future. The tubes 'lower' or 'raise' objects out of the past from a fixed point. Removing matter from one time to another is a very dangerous undertaking. All neighboring space is strained and distorted until replacements are effected. We yielded the information necessary to the construction of the tubes with the greatest reluctance and only under the most rigid conditions. A key man was required to sacrifice his life the moment he had completed the tubes.

"They cannot be duplicated.

"None of the other vessels from the past is equipped with explosive weapons, which is why they are of no help to the winged men. The groundmen, in constructing both cities, strove to protect them from energy weapons, first by direct defense, second by insuring that neither council ever gave out weapon information. This purpose was accidentally defeated when the seamen discovered a forgotten city, which had sunk into the sea thousands of years ago. In it, they found among other devices, the very powerful magnetic negator, now being used to drag the city of the winged men into the water.

"None of the instruments, such as the carrier used to transport the dead shark, will work outside the sea city, and the seamen do not know the secret of construction. All this was planned long ago by the groundmen.

"The fact that your commander is alive will make it necessary for you to recapture your ship, in order to prevent an ill-conceived attack on the city under the sea. At no time did we approve the alliance of the winged men with these creatures of the Sessa Clen. The attack, if it is finally made, will take all the bravery, skill, and intelligence of a first-class, highly integrated crew.

"What is more, it will have required that you make a decision, first as to whether or not you will attack the sea city, second, as to what in the city you will attack. You do not have the weapons necessary for the destruction of every compartment in that strongly walled city.

"We cannot influence your decision by hypnotism or other force. We have no force at our disposal. Therefore, we desire that, above everything else, your choice be freely made, perhaps under the pressure of events, but not forced in one direction by gracelessly selfish minds.

"One final suggestion, concerning the recapture of your

ship: Your weakness is your strength. Your ship has primitive aspects. The captors of it are bound to make a mistake, to believe somehow that it is better than it is."

Silence fell.

Then there was light, and then feeling.

Chapter 18

He was swinging at the end of a sling, being lowered to the deck of the *Sea Serpent*.

His feet touched the metal. He stood there, dazedly aware that Laren was removing the sling. He looked up in time to see the winged men retreating into the sky like a flock of frightened birds.

He looked down in time to see Dorilee climbing out of the hatch, anger in every line of her face. Observing her, the thought struck Kenlon: She's certainly changed since the takeover. He felt a strong detestation.

"Well, they kept you long enough," Dorilee greeted him acidly. "What did they do to you?"

Kenlon stared at her, puzzled. He had the feeling that he was not hearing correctly. At most he had been away only a few hours. How long did she think such a visit should take?

He parted his lips to say this. And it was at that moment that the astounding things that had happened to him struck through him. He closed his mouth with a click of his teeth. And stood there, stunned.

In a curious way, he expected the memory of it to fade. But after a minute it was still there, not a dream at all.

The woman was speaking again through clenched teeth:

"Your officers absolutely refused to co-operate with me in any way." Her eyes burned with a bright annoyance. Her lips were drawn into a straight uncompromising line.

Kenlon found his voice. "Naturally," he said curtly. "I am the commander. They will not act without orders from me."

The Tenant said with finality, "We're taking the ship down today whether we receive co-operation or not. If anything goes wrong, I am counting on your desire to save your submarine and your men, to insure that an incident does not become a disaster."

She went on furiously, "A whole day! Are the winged men mad that they permitted their council to keep you so long? I notice that they've been staying away from me, and that they permitted Nemmo to give me the location of the sea city. They must have no control over the situation at all and are ashamed of their helplessness. Well, they ought to be."

She finished with a rush: "What I'd like to know is, *what happened to you?*"

Twenty-four hours, Kenlon was thinking. It seemed impossible. Not one of the incarnations, not one of the fantastic episodes had seemed to last more than three-quarters of an hour. Add to that the time necessary for the journey up to and down from the eyrie and . . .

Three hours, not twenty-four—the logicalization of the sequence was not reassuring. He said slowly:

"I'd like to ask you a question, Tenant."

The tone of his voice must have been conciliatory, because the woman said quickly, and in an altered voice:

"Yes?"

"What did *you* see when you were taken before the council of the winged men?"

Dorilee looked at him with narrowed eyes, as if she were striving to extract special meaning from his question. She said abruptly:

"A roomful of energy tubes. The council is, of course, nothing but a machine made by the now long-dead groundmen. It is an extension of their accumulated knowledge, an automatic brain that knows everything. It has a pseudo-life, but it merely reacts to stimuli on the basis of careful pre-programing."

Kenlon absorbed that during a brief silence, then: "What happened?"

Dorilee looked at him. "To me, you mean? Why, the machine simply talked into my mind. It professed to find that our ship would not be useful to the winged men and dismissed me."

"Oh!" said Kenlon.

There seemed to be nothing at all that he could say to that. He grew aware that the woman was watching him grimly.

"Well," she said, "do you co-operate, or don't you?"

"Co-operate?" echoed Kenlon.

The parrotlike quality of his remark irritated him. But it was also startling to realize that all these minutes she had been standing there expecting him to say yes or no to her proposition, when actually he hadn't given it a thought.

With Jones-Gordon alive in the city of the fishmen, he could no more participate in an attack on that city than . . .

His mind poised there. Memory came of what the council had said: he would have to stop the attack. Not that he required the advice. The need for the counteraction grew out of the fact.

But it seemed important not to let the woman suspect the real reason. Kenlon said slowly:

"From your manner, I feel that you think I have had time to develop a more favorable attitude toward your reckless seizure of my ship. That is not the case. At the moment I have only one desire."

Explanations, it seemed to him, would but serve to confuse the issue. He finished coolly:

"If you have no objection, I would like to talk to Nemmo. I want to question him about what happened to me during my—interview—with the council."

The woman said sullenly, "You still have the neutralizer bar I gave you?"

Silently, Kenlon took it out of his pocket.

"Then go below!" she commanded.

A minute later, the engines were throbbing; and there was movement.

Everywhere below were Joannas. Kenlon counted twenty from glimpses he had through open doors, including three in the engine room and five in the stern torpedo room, his destination.

The possible total, if those farther forward were added, as they would have to be, shocked him. He had been so intent on seeing Nemmo that the problem of regaining control of the submarine had been pushed to the background of his mind. Now, it came to the fore; then receded quickly, defeated by the mere contemplation of the odds that were arrayed against success.

Nemmo was lying on the hammock that had been strung up for him a month before. He sat up when he saw Kenlon.

"I have been waiting for you," he said eagerly. "I was advised a little while ago that you had been returned to the ship."

He smiled in a friendly fashion, yet Kenlon noticed that there was anxiety in his manner. The winged man spoke again, urgently:

"The council kept your mind a long while. We have all been wondering what it showed you and told you. You will help us now, I hope."

Kenlon stared at the man. There was an empty feeling inside him. Nemmo's questions sounded as if there wasn't going to be any clarification from him. "See here," he began; then he explained swiftly what had happened, omitting only the part about his recapturing the submarine. He watched carefully for any revealing expression on the other's face.

There was much there to watch: puzzlement, amazement, disappointment, and, finally, when Kenlon came to the fact that Jones-Gordon was alive, sorrowful anger.

"You were told that!" Nemmo said in agitation. "Why, that could have only one result: that you would refuse to help us."

With a visible effort, he forced silence upon himself. He sat swaying in the hammock, his wings fluttering. He muttered finally:

"It is not that I wish ill to your commander. But the very existence of a race is at stake. Dozens of winged men have not returned from the time periods to which they were sent for weapons. Death has struck us in every direction; we are threatened by even greater destruction—and the council told you that!"

Once more he seemed to find it necessary to restrain himself by muscular force. Once more, after a pause, his voice came again at a quieter level. Grim and miserable, he said:

"All through this affair, the council has acted with reluctance, as if all its basic credos are at stake. We can understand that in a way. The council was originally constructed to consider both races. What is hard to understand is that in a crisis it has virtually betrayed us."

The winged man faced Kenlon appealingly. "I know that I have no right to ask you, but surely you can launch your torpedoes at vital points of the sea city without endangering your commander's life. I can guarantee that the council will reveal his exact position in the city."

"I wouldn't take the risk," Kenlon answered flatly.

He knew that he was being obstinate, even irrational. It probably could be done. But he knew, shakily, that it was more than just a matter of feasibility. He hadn't made up his mind about all this. That was the factor involved. The choice he was being called upon to make wasn't simply a case of evaluating between right and wrong.

The winged men *were* right—on one level. In spite of their hasty alliance with the Sessa Clen, he did not question their motives or their honesty for a single instant. But there was something to be said for the wrong side. There was the wonder and glory of life under the sea. Standing there, Kenlon felt the thrill of that swim, that fight with the shark. Human beings were involved in a new career in a savage and primitive environment. The prospect appealed to every atom of adventure in Kenlon's body.

Nor were the seamen alone in the universe with their cold logic. Memory came to Kenlon of all the conversations he had had with naval officers, many of whom advocated that, in time of war it was necessary to completely exterminate the enemy. There was no doubt of it, he personally came from an age where thoughts like that were steady, burning lights in the minds of gentle, kindly men who hated aggressors.

In this situation, the fishmen were the aggressors. It was hard, though, to think them absolutely wrong when the whole fate of man was involved, when the slightest mistake might result in man's disappearance from earth and from the universe.

Kenlon had a reluctant conviction that the fishmen would be better able to handle the Yaz. And if that were true . . .

He sighed. One thing was clear. He was not yet ready to make a decision.

There was a clang from above. Kenlon jumped. Then half-turned away from Nemmo. "They've closed the hatch," he said, alarmed. "They shouldn't have done that with—"

He stopped and bit his lip savagely to keep from saying the rest of the sentence.

What he had intended to say was that they shouldn't have battened down while the auxiliary engines were running. He didn't say it, for he was remembering what the council of the winged men had said, about his captors not understanding primitive machinery.

He whirled with a strong sense of urgency, then hurried farther forward to the tank he wanted to be near. He reached it, sank down beside it, and lay there, already beginning to gasp for breath.

One of the five Joannas who had been in the room had gone out a minute or so before; Kenlon recollected that vaguely now, lying there. The four who remained were beginning to stagger. They looked at each other in what must have been a hazy fashion; for their stumblings grew more pronounced, like blind men thrown off balance on a floor suddenly grown fantastically uneven.

Two of the women seemed simultaneously aware of Kenlon. They ran unsteadily toward him. One gasped something in her own language, saw that he didn't understand, swayed for a moment, and then both women seemed to forget him.

Clutching their throats, they tottered toward the doorway. All four seemed to have that purpose at the same moment. Three of the four got safely through and disappeared beyond Kenlon's field of vision. The fourth fell with the groping gentleness of a person overcome by insidious fumes.

The air near the floor had more oxygen in it; and, briefly, it seemed to revive her. But she had strained her body to the limit, fought too hard during those frantic minutes. And to make matters worse, she tried to get up.

She sank unconscious onto the floor. There would be others like her in every part of the ship, their purpose, all their will for life defeated by the primitive, ravenous engines, whose lust for air was so enormous that four or five minutes of monstrous gulping sufficed to exhaust the entire supply of a large submarine.

In the perfect submarine, of which their technical books must have told them, the problem of having auxiliary engines under water must have been solved without the use of air-breathing diesels.

And so they hadn't considered the need for oxygen.

Now that it had happened, it was obvious to Kenlon why they hadn't used the atomic-powered steam turbines. It was an indirect application of atomic energy, incredibly complex, a process of many steps. The Clen engineer had bypassed that problem, had utilized the simpler mechanism.

Kenlon reached that point in his automatic analysis and experienced a blackout. It was only partial, and he was able to reach up and turn on the valve of the oxygen tank. He quickly took a few life-giving breaths, then turned it off, and stood up. He walked, not ran, to the girl lying in the doorway.

He removed her energy rod from her belt, shoved it in his pocket, and walked on. There were five Joannas sprawling in the engine room. The highly adaptable engines were still running but coughing uncertainly now on their diet of almost pure oil. Kelon shut them off, hastily grabbed up the five energy rods from the belts of the women; and then, like a diver who has stayed under water too long, he hurried, pop-eyed, back to the oxygen tank.

This time the oxygen intoxicated him. But he retained enough sense to leave the tap open and to remember his purpose. A gentle hiss followed as he moved lightheartedly through the sub, removing energy guns from Joannas. There were altogether twenty-eight of the Sessa Clen's soldiers aboard including the Tenant, who was lying unconscious in the bridge.

Kenlon locked their rods in one of the lockers, then carried the Joannas one by one into the forward torpedo room. The various oxygen tanks he had turned on were suffusing the atmosphere with their life; the women were stirring as he grimly stripped them nude and left them.

It was a rude business, but there was no alternative. Some part of their clothing must make them immune to the neurals. He had to take every stitch to make sure that he got the neutralizing elements.

As he emerged from the torpedo room, Kenlon saw that some of his men had recovered and, what was more, were aware of what he was doing. For the first time it struck Kenlon that he had recouped his prestige. In that curious world of Navy men, this would be an exploit to be told in song and story—if it were ever told at all.

An hour later, when the *Sea Serpent* was again fully manned and heading back toward the eyrie, he was still lightheaded and lighthearted.

Tedders came up to the bridge. "The winged man wants to see you, sir."

"Very well."

Kenlon went below.

Nemmo greeted him gravely: "I have just been advised by my colleagues that your commander was brought to the surface by the fishmen a few minutes ago. He is alive and well."

Kenlon realized he felt relieved.

He sat in the motor launch and headed toward the shell that contained the commander. He could see that officer plainly now, through the transparent watertight plastic

bubble in which he had been brought up through the
water from the undersea city. His sense of relief grew. In
a few moments, chance would have removed the whole
problem of this age from his shoulders. As first officer
aboard the U.S. Submarine *Sea Serpent,* he would again
be subject to the orders of Lieutenant Commander
Jones-Gordon. For him, the time for choosing was over;
although, strangely enough, there was an idea, a solution,
in the back of his head, based on what he now knew
about this entire situation.

With a start he grew aware that a mass of winged men
were gliding down toward the launch. One of them came
very low. Kenlon recognized Laren. The winged man
shouted:

"The council . . . has asked us . . . to place ourselves
at your disposal. If there is anything we can do—"

There wasn't. Kenlon shook his head at them all even
while puzzlement came at the curious offer.

He forgot it and them.

He found himself wondering what the meeting with
Jones-Gordon would be like. He felt strangely on the
verge of exciting events.

The meeting proved quite unexciting. Jones-Gordon
climbed aboard and shook hands with Kenlon. Almost instantly, he drew Kenlon off to the rear seat. He said
sharply:

"What did those winged men want?"

"They offered their help, sir."

"Humph!"

Jones-Gordon sat scowling, then:

"There is no time to waste. I have been kept more or
less abreast of affairs by means of a very curious mind
device. Am I to understand our submarine was seized in
my absence by the winged men?"

Kenlon described briefly what had happened. When he
had finished, Jones-Gordon said:

"I never did trust those scoundrelly winged men."

"Eh!" said Kenlon. He was startled. It struck him that,
put into words, what the winged men had done sounded
far worse than the reality. He felt the necessity for ex-

plaining their actions. The queer conviction of impending
events was stronger. But somehow it no longer seemed
exciting. An odd, ugly thrill touched him.

He began: "Their situation was desperate. They apolo-
gized sincerely for what they were doing. They really
deserve sympathy. They—"

He was cut off. "Let me decide what they deserve."
Lieutenant Commander Jones-Gordon sat up very
straight. "I might as well tell you, Mr. Kenlon, that I have
made a deal with the fishmen. They will return us to our
time if we drop torpedoes onto that bird cage up there in
the sky, and knock it into the sea. I have agreed to do
so."

"WHAT?" said Kenlon.

Jones-Gordon went on as if he had not heard: "As
soon as we are aboard the *Sea Serpent,* you will have our
plane lowered. You will oversee the removal of the warheads from four of the new-type sectional torpedoes, and
make sure they are properly stowed in the bomb bay of
the plane. The machinery which supports the eyrie is at
the top of the building. Remove all unnecessary gasoline
from the plane's tanks. Flight Officer Orr will see to the
aiming!"

"But, sir—" Kenlon said.

He got no further. He couldn't. His mind was reeling
before the mad words he had heard; the utter, murderous
insanity of the words. Numbly, he fumbled for a verbal
weapon that would nullify what the other had said.

"But, sir—murdering those poor—"

"Nonsense!" The answer was brusque. "It is merely the
practical course that I have chosen. We had to ally ourselves with some group in this age. The winged men can
do us no harm.The fishmen can. So we work with them."

"The practical course!" said Kenlon bitterly. Once
again, the choking sensation silenced him. He sat sick and
cold with horror. He muttered at last:

"I must say, sir, for the first time in my career, I utterly
disapprove of your course of action."

He paused, shocked by his own words. It *was* the first
time. In all his naval career, he had never questioned,

never doubted. He had given advice only when it was asked, and accepted without a second thought every risk attendant on another man's decisions. Conscious now of his awful temerity, he nevertheless muttered grimly:

"This is murder, sir."

They were looking straight at each other now. Jones-Gordon was angry.

"Mr. Kenlon," he said curtly, "I'll have no more nonsense. We are confronted with a situation whereby a choice is necessary. We must decide between one or the other of two groups in this remote time world. My sole consideration, in making my decision, was to insure the return of our submarine to our own time."

"What you have done," said Kenlon, "will have the exact opposite effect. These fishmen have no time machines. They—"

He stopped. He recognized the stolid look that was settling over Jones-Gordon's heavy face. The officer was closing his mind to arguments. Here, weighted with the unimaginative character of the man, were the elements of utter ruin. Kenlon said, doggedly now:

"This may mean my rank, but I shall have nothing whatever to do with such a fantastic and unworthy plan."

The moment he had spoken, he knew that it wasn't enough. He couldn't just wash his hands of this, couldn't just look the other way while murder was done. For the second time within a space of hours, memory came of a phrase the council of the winged men had addressed to him:

We desire that your choice be made freely, made perhaps under the pressure of events but . . .

Never in all his life had the pressure of events been so great. If only he could have time out to think, some fraction of a day that would give him opportunity for the dignity of consideration.

But there was no time. Murder, cold-blooded murder was about to be done. And only prompt action could avert it.

Quite suddenly, Kenlon knew what that action must be—in all its details. He glanced with a measuring eye toward the submarine. It was still about three hundred yards away. They had hove-to at a good distance, fearing a trap.

Extremely tense now, Kenlon glanced up at the winged men. They had been winging along at the upper edge of his vision. There were about a hundred of them, approximately two hundred feet up.

In that exalted moment of decision, he had not the faintest doubt but that the council, the omniscient council of the winged men, had anticipated this moment, this very situation—and had told them. And that they would react to his slightest action.

Kenlon stood up, and *looked* up.

The reaction was faster than his anticipation. Winged men came swooping down. Kenlon shouted at them, articulating the necessary commands.

Jones-Gordon was on his feet. "Hells bells!" he said. "What are you saying to them?"

"I'm telling them to get away, sir. They look as if they're about to attack."

There was no question about that. He had ordered them to seize Jones-Gordon.

The next second everybody aboard was prisoner, their guns tossed aboard, their arms, their bodies, their legs held by strong, muscular hands.

"Hold me, too!" Kenlon shouted.

And he was held.

Laren came over to him. "What shall we do with your commander?"

"Return him to the submarine when I tell Nemmo."

There were many things to do. First, send the Joannas back to their ship; then visit Arpo . . .

Chapter 19

As he came close to the blue craft, Kenlon kept expecting that his mind would be contacted by the telepathic method that had been so sensationally perfect that first time.

When that didn't happen, he felt an excitement. Was it possible . . . he was welcome?

When his little boat was still a score of feet away, a man in loose, silken-like clothing came on deck and waved at him in a genial fashion. He was large and blond, and—Kenlon saw—a beautiful physical specimen.

The stranger reached down, caught Kenlon's hand in his own with a firm grip, and pulled him aboard.

At close range, he seemed even more magnificent appearing. His head was leonine; he radiated personal power.

A thought formed in Kenlon's mind; the first mental communication: "Welcome aboard, fellow human. Be my guest forever."

That was the meaning. But there was an overtone of good feeling, which implied: "Go freely, come freely, do freely."

As Kenlon asked to go below, he thought: Is it possible that people have always had the potentiality for giving out love in such quantities without restrictions?

The inside of Arpo's ship was splendidly engineered. There were deep, comfortable chairs. At some unseen command from Arpo, the chair nearest Kenlon swiveled around. Then a nearby chair turned to face it. As Kenlon sank into the one indicated by his host, Arpo walked over and sat down opposite him.

The two men—the submarine officer in his neatest white uniform, and the superman from the twentieth millennium in what looked like pajamas—sat looking at each other.

"You see what's in my mind?" Kenlon said.

Arpo said that he did, and that as a precaution he had already put an energy block around Kenlon, so that the Yaz would not be able to monitor this and the other visits that he planned.

Arpo's thought continued: "The problems presented by these aliens cannot be dealt with simply."

Kenlon waited, almost not daring to breathe.

Arpo's thought went on: "Beings like the Yaz have an entirely subjective feeling in favor of their own kind and will not change until innumerable interactions among the different races of the galaxy have occurred. It is only after many clashes and dialogues through the centuries ahead that we shall come to a condition out in space paralleling what finally happened on Earth, when my ancestors made a successful stand against war and violence.

"No such opportunity exists out in the stars at present. Naturally, I shall help you . . ."

From Arpo's ship, Kenlon went to the high-masted fishing vessel. After Kenlon had explained what he wanted to Robairst, the man went below. When he came on deck again, he was grim. "Tainar will remain aboard," he said. "I'll go over to your submarine. We think your plan is good."

It was Arpo's plan, but Kenlon did not correct the other man's impression. Proper credits could be given later.

Kenlon went next to the *Segomay 8*. He found Captain Gand to be a sturdily built man about fifty years old. Gand listened for a few moments; then: "Just a minute," he said into his microphone. "I think everybody ought to hear this."

A minute later, Kenlon was explaining about the Yaz. If there was any response from the men below, no feedback was offered to him.

When Kenlon finished his account, Gand said, "Commander, we had a lie detector reading you while you spoke, and your account is true. We agree to your plan and will be ready about 2 A.M. tonight to carry out our part of an attack."

He shook hands presently with Kenlon; his eyes were bright. "Changes things, doesn't it? I'm scared. But I'm impressed that Arpo is going along with it, though just what he can do is not clear to me."

"He told me he could penetrate into their ship," Kenlon said.

Gand's eyes grew wide. "By himself?"

"Mentally."

"Oh!" Gand was silent, then: "I don't understand it. But it sounds impressive. Did he say what he could do when he got there?"

"No."

"Well—" doubtfully. "We'll just have to hope for the best. This is certainly an unexpected development," he finished, his heavy face pale.

"We're listening in," said a voice.

"Huh!" said Gand.

He looked around, startled, then glanced at the speaker instrument.

"This is Tulgoronet, Commander Kenlon and Captain Gand."

. . . One of the men from the round ship, Kenlon recognized after a moment. He said, "You've improved your method of communication."

Gand interjected quickly, addressing Kenlon: "You know what this is?"

Kenlon explained. Then they were both silent as the Setidillad leader continued:

"Yes, we've been working long hours. We can now tune in on the intercom systems of the various ships and utilize their translation computers. We thought we'd save you the trouble of coming over here."

It was getting late, and Kenlon appreciated the consideration.

"We also transmitted your explanation to the Sessa Clen's ship," said Tulgoronet. "They will co-operate."

Kenlon was relieved. The royal atmosphere of the Clen ship was oppressive to him and he had not looked forward to a visit there.

Tulgoronet went on, puzzled, "Something radiates from you. It wasn't there before. Did those lizard people do anything to you?"

Kenlon was startled, but he answered honestly, "I've given you an accurate account."

On the way back to the *Sea Serpent,* he braced himself against the fear that Tulgoronet's words had brought.

Chapter 20

The battle that was fought that night probably had no parallel in the history of the world.

The attacking fleet consisted of the *Segomay 8*—a thousand-foot-long sea-mining maintenance freighter from the twenty-ninth century—a fishing vessel from the forty-third century, a space research ship from about A.D. 10,-000, a pleasure yacht from the Clen civilization of around A.D. 13,000, a small craft with one male—Arpo—from the two-hundredth century, AND a submarine—the U.S.S. *Sea Serpent* commanded by William Kenlon—from an early, primitive mechanical era.

The enemy was a single supership from a civilization that had its home planet in the Milky Way.

Kenlon was assigned over-all command. In the conning tower of his craft there now sat three new crew members, and some equipment that no twentieth-century U.S. submarine had ever had: a translating relay system that connected with the *Segomay 8* and the round ship, an energy unit from the round ship which could set up a protective field, a remote control device for manipulating the automatic machinery of the Sessa Clen's yacht, and a control unit for the fishing weapons aboard Robairst's and Tainar's vessel.

The new crew members were Robairst from the fishing vessel, Massagand from the round ship, and a Joanna whom Kenlon had not seen before—she had been introduced as the assistant engineer of the Clen ship, and she was undoubtedly the most advanced scientifically trained person on the submarine.

Shortly after midnight, Kenlon received a mental com-

munication from Arpo that all was ready, and he thereupon gave the order for the attack.

In the darkness, all the vessels now converged on the
alien.

Exactly when the Yaz became aware that something
was afoot could never be precisely established. But suddenly the night began to brighten. It quickly took on a
peculiar daylight appearance—peculiar in that it was a
soft light, like a sun shining through fleecy clouds; only
there was no bright area to indicate the presence of a sun.

The daylike brightness extended for well over a mile.
Then it grew softer, duller, fading away at a rate that was
much faster than the square of the distance. So it was not
a one-source phenomenon.

Kenlon mentally asked Arpo about it. The answer
came: "They are using the atmosphere as, in your age,
you utilize a neon gas. The massiveness of the action
derives from a technique whereby an electron is alter-
nately negative and positive, thus it can theoretically be
re-used an infinite number of times for the same purpose.
In practice, of course, there is some leakage. Otherwise
the brightness would continue to increase—"

It was bright enough. The submarine, with only its
periscope showing, continued its forward drive, as did the
Segomay 8, the fishing vessel, and the round ship.

There was no immediate further action by the Yaz.
The dark, curved, surface structure of their cigar-shaped
craft remained only slightly above water. It showed no
sign of moving or even of starting to move.

Kenlon's awareness of the alien must have been maintained by Arpo, for a thought came: "Don't be misled.
The time lapse between motion and no-motion in such
an advanced ship will be a matter of milliseconds. And
at the critical moment they will use the power they
established over you."

Kenlon was startled. "What power?" he asked.

Having spoken, he felt a fear of the unknown, a sense
of being helpless in the grip of superior forces.

Arpo's thought was calm: "You went to their ship.
They fired a capsule into your body. It's there now."

"I felt nothing," said Kenlon. But he realized from the numbness in his face that all surface color had drained from his cheeks. And he realized, too, that this must be what Tulgoronet had vaguely detected.

With an effort, he caught himself. "I shouldn't be commander of this task force," he said. "Perhaps I should try to leave the submarine."

Arpo remained calm. "It's all or nothing. It will be a matter of fine timing whether or not we win. Meanwhile, logically, they won't quickly destroy your submarine, which they hope to have you use against the fish people. They have no inkling yet that I have involved myself in the battle. I plan to reveal this in a few moments. Would you care to come along?"

"You mean, sort of mentally?"

His question must have had in it his acquiescence; for abruptly he was inside the Yaz ship.

Four of the lizard men had somehow turned to face them all in a flash, and Kenlon was vaguely aware that lights flickered around his head—tiny brightnesses that seemed mere points but were as hard and brittle as gems.

Then he was back in the sub. Kenlon stood for a moment, dazed; then he took a deep breath; then, "What happened?" he asked.

"They threw us out!" was the mental reply from Arpo. "But now they know."

It seemed a fruitless act; it was hard to believe that what had happened had served any useful purpose. The mystery of Arpo's participation might better have been kept a secret—so it seemed to Kenlon.

"No!" whispered Arpo's mind into his. "The first act of a battle has to occur sooner or later. It has now occurred. It was a great shock to them."

Kenlon gave up. His view of the matter was clearly incomplete, for he tended to consider that the best weapons should be used with total power and total surprise.

Now, the surprise was gone, and not a single shot—so to say—had been fired.

He had the unhappy feeling that Arpo, the man of peace, was too unfamiliar with war to realize that the rules were: When you strike, strike to kill. No preliminary conversations. No requests for surrender. In war, one tried for victory right now.

Arpo's thought came: "I can't permit you to hold such a negative concept of me, Commander. When you and I went in there, it was to kill. I told you—they threw us out."

"You mean, we were defeated?"

"Yes—in a manner of speaking. It was four against one, and they were on the point of using my projective energy to strike at me in my ship, at which point, I withdrew. So it was a defeat in the sense that an attack which could have ended the battle, was unsuccessful. It was not a defeat in the sense that they were able to follow and destroy me."

Kenlon was trying to visualize the engagement as he had observed it. He remembered the hard, bright points of light around his head. Remembering, he shivered slightly in retrospective anxiety. For there seemed no question the points of light represented mighty forces.

What staggered him, as he strove to recollect the moment to moment happenings, was the great speed at which everything had happened.

If there was such a thing as instant battle, that had been it.

Shakily, he asked: "What do we do now?"

"Keep moving closer."

Closer they moved. When the submarine was half a mile from the Yaz spaceship, the aliens emitted a long, glowing, white object that looked like a burning rope. The "rope" curved toward the *Segomay 8* like some strange fireworks. Instants before it would have struck, the entire rope disappeared.

Arpo's thought came to Kenlon: "I'm holding that energy complex out of phase. Now, here's what you do. Tell the *Segomay 8* to put a pressor beam on the Dika—that's what the Yaz call their spaceship—I'll wait till you've done that."

The order was hastily transmitted to Gand, who yelled back: "Pressor on target!"

"Now," telepathed Arpo, "have the Sessa Clen's ship insert sea water into that pressor."

"B-but," Kenlon argued, "when they did that before, it was with a tractor beam."

"But then the water went *to* the *Segomay 8*. This time we want to put it into the Dika. Your Joanna engineer will understand."

When Kenlon transmitted that message, the woman's eyes brightened. She pushed a button. "That other time, we were gentle, we didn't want to hurt anybody. Now, we'll really let them feel it. Watch the alien."

As Kenlon watched, the Yaz ship sank out of sight. He waited anxiously. But the seconds passed, and the Dika did not reappear.

"What happened?" he asked silently of Arpo.

"They're three-quarters full of water. And although they come from a water culture, in going out into space they had to eliminate all unnecessary mechanisms. Right now, they are down about twenty feet below surface, and they have no quick way of getting rid of the water. I sense that they have some plan, but it's not clear. They may try to leave. So alert Massagand and no matter what happens, he must not leave his station."

Grimly, Kenlon transmitted this command; and then, as he turned back to the periscope, it occurred to him that perhaps the solution to all this would be to let the Yaz get away.

This thought transformed somehow into a feeling, a warm and intimate sense of wanting the correct thing to happen in this trying situation. He became aware of sounds not too far away. He seemed to have drifted away from the interior of the sub into some kind of mist.

The first thing Kenlon became aware of was a faint, faraway roaring, as of water pounding and surging on a near rocky shore.

Then he saw that he was in deep water, swimming. The water was warm, and he was strong and it was great to be alive in this mighty ocean. And then he saw that he was not alone. Other lizard-men—several hundred—were in the water near him, around him.

He knew—without thinking about it—that he was on his home planet, and that he and his companions were having one of their continuing discussions about the future.

The one true race had been moving into the universe for a long time, and this must be accelerated. More and more of them must go farther and farther. The water homeland, and all the planets already taken over were fantastically overpopulated.

And, actually, their going out, their taking over the universe was a good thing. They were the true life of time and space; they had the true way, the true and perfect bodies. A complete being existed at last, and they were it.

It was not a spoken thought, that belief. It went deep indeed and need not be stated in any way. Their feeling about themselves had a simple, pure reality, and needed no words or reassurance.

Since nature had, in the Yaz, produced perfection, no other race was actually needed. Of course, most non-water races could be tolerated; they didn't matter, or have any value one way or another. But they need not be a problem. Perfection could accept the presence or existence of imperfection, perhaps as a reminder of the way things had once been. . . .

The scene changed. He was looking out at a number of vessels converging on the Yaz ship. Without thinking about it—as Kenlon—he recognized the Sessa Clen's yacht, the *Segomay 8,* the submarine periscope, the round ship, and the smaller craft.

—And he knew what he must do. Sink them all. The simplest solution was for the submarine to launch six perfectly aimed torpedoes.

Don't let anyone stop him!

—Kenlon came to consciousness with a start. He was being held by Robairst, Benjamin, the chief electrical officer and his assistant. He was struggling desperately, yelling at them. Only Massagand remained at his post.

Abruptly, he realized the truth. Instantly, he ceased his fighting.

"I'm all right now," he gulped breathlessly. "Just keep an eye on me."

They all got to their feet. Robairst said into his little microphone, "Arpo warned us. He says you are all right for the moment, but that it's not over."

"Quick!" came Arpo's thought into Kenlon's mind. "Everybody back to stations. They're trying to take advantage of the confusion to get away."

Massagand called to Kenlon. "Look!" he said.

Kenlon stepped over and glanced down at the indicated dials. One needle was wavering. Another was spinning slowly. A third had moved from a zero position almost to the extreme opposite side.

One look only Kenlon took at that; and then he stepped back and peered through the periscope—barely in time to see the finale of that action. The Dika was up out of the water, a cigar-shaped structure. It was slowly climbing. As he watched, it rose about five hundred feet, and then it seemed to pause.

"It's caught in our field," Massagand's voice came. "Everything seems to be at peak right now. That's an experimental field that we used to slow meteorites in their orbits, and we handled several with it that were over ten miles in diameter. That ship cannot possibly have that much lifting power, so in a moment—"

The moment passed; and the Yaz ship began to fall.

"While it's in that helpless condition," came Massagand's voice, "we'll twist the field around and wreck their machinery and smash the walls of their ship."

"Come with me!" said Arpo's thoughts in Kenlon's mind.

Instantly, he was inside the Dika.

—It was a scene that Kenlon would never forget. But one that he had visualized many times in his more shuddery moments. For what he saw in the alien was the submariner's nightmare.

—Utter disaster! The water was almost up to the ceiling. And as the ship turned over and over in its fall, the gigantic liquidy mass of it surged with incredible violence through the interior of the doomed vessel.

From all sides came the screeching sound of metal tearing and breaking.

Once again, Kenlon thought in horror: This is what it's like when a submarine is hit. Water roars in, engines break loose; and the whole screaming, ripping mass goes down . . .

Yet, after that thought had come, he saw a lizard-man somehow flattened against one wall, undamaged, watching with those alert eyes, evaluating. As a wall of water surged toward the creature man, he turned his head to avoid its blow, and when the water was past, there he still was, alert, watching.

Thinking.

It was only a brief glimpse that Kenlon had, but it left him uneasy.

The next second, he was back in the submarine.

Arpo's thought came: "There are still enough of them there. I didn't wait to find out if they could throw us out, because they're now trying to explode the capsule inside you."

"Oh!" Kenlon said.

He fought the fear that came; felt himself drained of color, whispered: "I should get out of the submarine, quick!"

"Wait!" came Arpo's stark command. "Tell Massagand to keep twisting that energy field, keep on wrecking their machinery."

Kenlon, pale, his voice hollow in his own ears, spoke the words.

The man from the round ship promised, "I'll sweep their vessel from stem to stern."

Kenlon watched the needles tensely. But it was he himself who registered the change. Deep inside him, something let go.

Not until he had the sensation of release did he realize that he had been aware of a tension in his solar plexus.

"That's it!" Arpo reported. "You're free. But the battle isn't over yet."

Kenlon watched through the periscope as the Dika struck.

The entire ocean heaved. Water splashed hundreds of feet. A wave that resembled a small mountain surged out in a circular ripple and rolled toward the little fleet of vessels.

After several seconds, the shattering roar of the big ship striking the water came through the speaker system like the explosion of a giant depth charge.

When that huge sound had died away, Kenlon hastily urged that a warning be sent out for all the ships to secure themselves against the tidal wave that was rolling in every direction.

Less than a minute later, the wave struck.

Although the submarine was at periscope depth and heading directly into the wave, the great ship heaved and shuddered, sank many yards, bounced until it surfaced, sank again, wallowed, trembled—but gradually resumed its course.

The other vessels were evidently sturdily built, for there they were when Kenlon finally was able to look.

"Wait!" said Arpo's thought.

Kenlon waited. The slow seconds went by. Then:

"They've abandoned ship," said Arpo. "They're going to find a remote undersea area where they can stay alive and build another ship."

Kenlon waited uneasily.

Finally Arpo telepathed: "Tell Robairst to have Tainar fire twenty-two of those fish-hunting capsules around the area where the Dika crashed."

Tensely, Robairst transmitted the order.

Nearly a minute went by; then Tainar's voice sounded harshly: "All twenty-two fired."

"Wait!" That was Arpo again.

Finally his thought came through once more: "One of those hit a passing fish. Tell Tainar to fire another."

When that had been done, when another minute had gone by, Arpo gave the final order:

"Tell Tainar to explode all of them."

It was getting darker outside. The leakage on the Yaz aerial lighting system was evidently bringing about a gradual diminution of the process now that it was no longer reinforced from the alien's ship.

. . . Soon, there would be normal night.

Despite the developing dimness, Kenlon saw through the periscope the spots of bright water-surge as the repercussions from those explosions hit the surface. Each burst up with a huge splash that sent water as high as fifty or sixty feet.

He was unable to count if there were twenty-two; it was too fast, there were too many of them, too quickly. But presently came the anticipated reassurance.

"Congratulations, Commander," Arpo telepathed. "The battle is over. The enemy is destroyed. Man has his planet back."

Kenlon asked in anguish, "But what about the winged men and the fishmen? What's your choice between them?"

"No choice. Both are human."

"But I need help. I need some advice."

". . . Sorry . . . No help from me there. And now, goodbye, Commander Kenlon. I shall not be available for further communication."

"Wait—"

But no more thought waves came.

Kenlon turned slowly to face the others; and in his mind a decision was forming. He knew what it was; and it was not a completely fair thing. But his whole body was overstimulated from the battle that had barely come to its grim end.

It was the kind of moment when fighting men made decisions.

And for better or worse, the decision had come; and in this moment of body excitement, it seemed right.

Chapter 21

It was little more than an hour later that Kenlon gave the first of the deadly commands:

"Fire one!"

It took time, what he did then. He had his plan to adhere to, his solution. He kept returning to the same position, always firing through walls previously torn by the savage and unerring warheads of the monster torpedoes. It took twenty-six of their forty-eight torpedoes to reach the central core, where the council of the seamen were sheltered, and to smash that tremendous source of their knowledge.

When he finally ordered the *Sea Serpent* away, he left behind him a city 95 percent intact, but for all aggressive purposes, headless.

The seamen were still alive, but their ability to misuse science was ended for a measurable period. They would have to learn co-operation. In future, if they wanted scientific information, they must get it from the winged men.

But first—two more torpedoes for the electronic negator that was tugging with its silent power, striving to drag the eyrie into the sea . . . then say goodbye.

Through Tulgoronet, Kenlon made final contact with the other ships and made his farewells. When he called the Clen ship, surprisingly, the Sessa herself talked to him.

"Commander Kenlon," she said, through the translating mechanism, "I have genuine admiration for your behavior throughout your stay here. Watching you in action, it struck me forcibly that we don't have men of such courageous caliber in our own age. Indeed, I have—because of seeing you—decided not to go through with the marriage arranged for me in Clen. So"—suddenly she seemed a little embarrassed—"why don't you, when your commanding officer returns, come back with me to Clen time?"

It took a long moment for Kenlon to grasp the possible import of the request . . . a personal interest in him.

Briefly, in his mind's eye, he visualized the atmosphere of obedience to royalty in Greater Clen, pictured himself there, stultifying, and shuddered.

"My dear lady," he said gently, "people belong in their own eras, I in mine, you in yours."

After the connection was broken, Kenlon sat silent, thinking: What a fantastic universe. For a few days, people normally separated by the barriers of time, had mingled.

Soon, an immensity of years would rush between them.

. . . For all life purposes, it was forevermore.

Jones-Gordon was lowered to the bridge in a sling. He released himself with a brisk movement.

"See that everybody gets below, Mr. Kenlon," he said quietly. "We shall submerge to a depth of two hundred feet for safety. We are to be returned at once to our own time."

Nemmo came over and shook hands with Kenlon. "Our council was cleverer than all of us," he said.

Kenlon turned slowly to face his skipper. They were alone on the bridge, and they measured each other with steady glances. There was no question in Kenlon's mind that the lieutenant commander knew that he had mutinied.

Slowly, Jones-Gordon put out his hand.

"It looks to me, Bill," he said, "as if, when it comes to finding your way around in a crazy world, you've got a more practical mind than I have. You must have, because you were right."

They came up ten minutes after that, 24,999 years into the past. They came up into the brilliant sunshine of a South Pacific morning, and looked out on a calm and glittering sea.

Outstanding science fiction and fantasy

To order these titles,

see coupon on the

last page of this book.

A. E. VAN VOGT

in DAW Editions: